D0089882

MARY'S
Song

*Twelve-year-old Mary is determined to overcome her
limitations and change the destiny of a helpless foal
that has no hope and no future without her.*

Dream Horse Adventures – Book 1

Text Copyright © 2016 Susan Count

Illustrations by Ruth Sanderson
Book formatting and conversion by BookCoverCafe.com

Library of Congress Control Number: 2016940445

All Rights Reserved. No part of this text may be transmitted, reproduced, downloaded, or electronically stored without the express written permission of Susan Count.

This is a work of fiction. The names, characters, places and story incidents or actions are all products of the author's imagination. Any resemblance to actual persons, living or dead, events or locales, is entirely coincidental.

ISBN: 978-0-9970883-3-5 (pbk)
978-0-9970883-3-8 (ebk)

Dedication

This book is dedicated to my grandmother Charlotte Dann Count, librarian at the David M. Hunt Library in Falls Village, Connecticut (1948-58). She instilled in me the love of reading when she shelved all the classic horse books for me to discover.

To my amazing SCBWI critique group, The Critters.

Major kudos to my fantastic editor:
Deirdre Lockhart – Brilliant Cut Editing.

Thanks to my husband, David, daughter, Sarah, and son, Christopher, for the constant encouragement.

Glory to God. May the works of my hands
bring honor to the house of the Lord.

Dear Reader:

Please share a review of this book.
Check my website for any ongoing contests or giveaways.
http://www.susancount.com/

E-mail a comment:
susancountauthor@yahoo.com

Follow Susan Count
www.facebook.com/susancount
https://www.pinterest.com/susancount/
https://twitter.com/SusanCount

Mary's Song

Dream Horse Adventures
Book 1

Susan Count

CHAPTER ONE

In the year 1952

*M*aybe today?" Twelve-year-old Mary gripped the arm of her wheelchair with one hand and the bedrail with the other. Her weight balanced on the edge of the bed, and she inched forward onto her feet. Her legs trembled and buckled. As her knees slammed onto the wood floor, she grabbed desperately for the dresser, but snatched instead the crocheted covering. When it ripped away from the dresser top, her favorite carved horse sailed across the room, careening into the wall. One of the Morgan mare's legs and its ornately carved black tail snapped off as it ricocheted under the bed.

Ignoring the pain in her knees, she lifted the bed skirt. The rest of the disfigured horse lay out of her reach. Already sprawled across the floor, she scooted to retrieve the severed pieces and cradled them in her hands. "I have to hide you."

Papa would be so angry if he saw Mama's horse was broken. Heavy footsteps rushed toward her.

"Lame and worthless. Just like me." She slipped the broken horse into her skirt pocket. She struggled and strained to pull herself up off the floor, but collapsed as Papa burst into her room.

"What happened? I heard a commotion... Mary?" He dropped to his knee beside her. "What happened? Are you hurt?"

"I lost my balance when I tried to stand. I'm fine."

"Let's get you off the floor, shall we?" He lifted and placed her on the bed. "I think it would be best to call the doctor."

"I'm fine!" Mary said a little louder than she intended. "The hot rock therapy didn't help."

Papa sat on the bed and took her hand. "Don't give up. We'll find a therapy, my Mary. We'll never stop trying." He patted her hand. "You sure you're all right? Maybe you should lie down."

"I said I'm fine." But she looked out the window instead of into his eyes. She would never be all right. "Can you take me outside now?"

"If you're sure. Let's get you out in some fresh air." He dropped a paper-wrapped bundle of carrot pieces in her lap.

Mary tucked her long dark hair behind her ears. Gathering her sketchpad and pencils to her chest, she drew a deep breath and nodded.

In a practiced motion, he slung her blanket over his shoulder and scooped her from the bed.

"I want to believe I'll walk someday, but sometimes, I just can't." She tossed him a hint of a smile. He carried her through the colonial house, past the white porch pillars, and across the field. He was so strong it made her feel safe. He was certainly the most handsome papa in all the world.

The white oak had not leafed yet, so he placed her blanket in the shade of the pines out of the warm Texas sun. Mary smoothed her skirt and spread her art materials. "You were right about throwing carrots over the fence to bring the mares closer." She retrieved an art pencil hidden in the folds of her blanket. "Look. Here they come." She pointed with her pencil. "They see me and gallop like crazy to get here. The foals buck and kick the whole way. Our new neighbors are so lucky. I'd like to have a pasture full of Morgan horses."

"At least you get to enjoy them. I have to go now." He kissed the top of her head. "Have a nice day. Mr. Joe is working in the gardens, so when you're ready to go back to the house, holler for him."

"Will you be gone long?"

His face tensed, and his dark eyebrows pulled together. He looked over the meadow, frowning. "Only a few days this time."

"I wish you didn't always have to go. I miss you so much."

"I know it's hard on you. If it makes you feel any better, I don't like leaving you either. But I have business in New Orleans, and then I'm going to Destin, Florida. A doctor there thinks he can help you."

Her temper flared, and she slashed a big ugly squiggle across the sketchpad. "Not another one, Papa! You thought the medicine man would be the miracle cure. He danced and chanted and kept me in a dumb teepee for two days. Magic smoke. And for what?"

"Well... it wasn't one of my better ideas."

"I thought Mrs. Tate was going to faint when you told her where we'd been. She walked around the house all day shaking her feather duster and muttering 'pagan gods', something about never taking another day off, and praying real loud to God asking him to forgive you."

3

"Glad I missed that, but I'm not giving up. I'll consider any opportunity to heal you." He straightened his vest and tucked his thumbs in its little pockets. "If this technique can offer us hope, we have to try. The clinic would float you in emerald-colored seawater. Then they'd take you to the 'Fountain Of Youth'."

Her shoulders slumped with an exhale. "I don't need to get any younger. I need to walk."

"And walk you shall. That is just the name given to the spring by the explorer who discovered it." He patted her hand. "Sketch me several poses of the filly beside the dappled gray mare while I'm gone. What is it about her that always draws my eye?"

"She's special! I sketch her the most. The other foals will scatter, but she seems to want to be with me. If she was on this side of the fence, I think she'd be in my lap." Mary flipped to a clean paper. "It's her eyes. Our souls connect when our eyes meet. Don't you think they look like dark chocolate?" Mary warmed at the thought. "She is my favorite. What a character. She hides behind her mama sometimes and plays hide and seek with me." A frown wiped the smile off her face. "I think there might be something wrong. She limps sometimes."

Papa checked his watch and frowned. "Hum, that can't be good. Say, when I get home, I will have a little something special I ordered for you. Don't ask me what it is and ruin the surprise."

"No fair! Is it a book on the Lipizzaners?"

"You're a bad guesser."

"Whatever it is, I'll love it."

Papa grinned, tossed a piece of chocolate in her lap, and left.

"Thanks!" She waved and sailed a few carrot offerings over the fence to the gathered herd. They rushed to grab the bribe. With ears flattened, the horses jostled, shoved, and charged at one another to gobble the carrots. When the treats were gone, the mares went back to grazing. As the foals cavorted in circles around their dams, Mary inhaled the delight of being in their company. To draw a foal, she took a snapshot with her mind and sketched it in a great flurry. After capturing the likeness, she fussed with the details and the shading. A twine-wrapped portfolio she kept in her library bulged with sketches. Each sketch was a secret wish to ride, wild and free, someday.

She imagined herself cantering across a meadow polka-dotted with pink flowers. Her hair streamed behind her. Her arms held wide as if to soar. Her dream horse moved in response to her thoughts. A smile lifted and softened her face.

Mary shifted her useless legs to balance the sketchpad better. "It's not just a dream." The filly cocked her feminine head to the side and peered at the curiosity in the grass. Mary stared back, hoping the filly would hold the pose long enough for her to soak in every detail. The dark graphite pencil seemed to flow on its own, and soon the rough outline of the curious baby splashed across the paper.

"I will sketch you every minute until Papa comes home with my surprise. It might be—could be—a horse."

CHAPTER TWO

Two miles away at the neighboring horse farm, twelve-year-old Laura groaned and clutched the bedcovers as she dreamed.

Her knees dug into the sides of a galloping stallion. Its mane whipped in the torrent of wind. "Whoa," she begged with no effect on the raging animal.

The pounding thunder in her ears was the hoof beats of the red goliath. The beast leaped a gorge and landed amid slippery, loose shale. Rocks rattled as they scattered and plunged into great darkness below. The horse galloped down a narrow ledge mirroring the turns of the gorge. Ahead the ledge disappeared, but the horse surged forward. It gathered itself and sprung with a leopard's grace off the rocky cliff. Far below, great sharp stones and boulders jutted like spikes waiting to impale her. Laura's grip on the stallion's mane slipped, and she lurched off the horse. As the fire-red stallion landed on an outcropped ledge and disappeared into a cave, Laura tumbled through the air toward her doom. Her mouth opened in a scream, wrenching her soul awake.

She bolted upright in her bed, still screaming. Quick sharp breaths punctuated her bursts of fear. Fear of falling. Fear no one would come to save her. Fear of the dangerous, red, mysterious horse that carried her away in the night.

Clamping her hands over her mouth to stop screaming, she sucked in as much air as she could. As she held her breath, shiny spots flickered in her eyes, and she drifted toward blacking out. Soft as a kitten, Laura mewed, "Mama! I need you."

No footsteps rushed to comfort her. The grand house endured in silence while her heart pounded.

Dazed, she sat cross-legged on her bed and stared at the herd of Morgan mares grazing in the Bermuda grass. Their foals stretched out asleep nearby. All was right in their world.

Though she knew better, she hoped her mother was still in her bedroom. The polished stone floor chilled her feet as she hurried down the quiet hall. Mother's duvet cover laid tossed back and her big bed empty. She would already be in the barn. No need to bother looking for Father. He would have been long gone—off to attend to some business or other. Or just off to get a newspaper, but always gone.

Mary lifted her orange juice glass and propped her elbows on the smooth oak table. The morning sun warmed the huge kitchen as it filtered through yellow curtains splashed with itsy-bitsy white daisies with yellow centers. The five-foot-tall, full-figured housekeeper sprinkled the breadboard with a flour dust cloud. Kneading the sweet bread was a full-body workout for her.

"Mrs. Tate? I so miss Papa. He'll be home soon, right?"

Mrs. Tate wiped flour from her thick hands onto her apron. "After your school lessons, I should think." She cupped Mary's face and kissed her cheek before sidling back to the breadboard.

"He has a surprise for me. Will it be delivered today or is he bringing it with him?"

"You'll not trick me into telling you anything. I know your ways." She punched down the dough and sprinkled it with more flour. "Your sweetness is a disguise for a devious mind," Mrs. Tate teased.

Mary plopped her hands on her chest, threw her head back, and held her mouth open as if she had been stabbed. "My feelings are crushed. Anyway, I'm sure Papa found me a new book for my collection."

"You already have more books about horses than any library."

"My favorites I read over and over again. The pages are falling out of *The Crooked Colt.*" Mary plucked an apple from a copper bowl and dropped it into her lap. "Unless? Wouldn't it be amazing if Papa brought me a horse of my own? I'll bet that's his surprise. He really went to Florida to pick out a horse for me." She looked expectantly at Mrs. Tate for a sign that she had guessed correctly.

"You're dreaming. I wish you were fascinated with flowers or birds. Horses are much too dangerous for a young girl in your condition."

"I don't know how or when, but I know I'm not always going to be stuck in this chair. I'm going to ride horses someday, and I'm going to train them too."

Mrs. Tate's brow wrinkled. "Scoot along now to your lesson." She waved her finger in the direction of the hall. "Mr. Gregory is waiting."

Mary rolled her chair away from the table and pushed the wheels over the wooden plank flooring. "When I can walk,

I won't have to spend the day with someone who smells like a stale cigar. I'll go to a real school and have friends."

"Oh, Mary, my dear, I pray that over you every day."

"He's not listening to you." Mary's gaze followed the pink stripes of her cotton skirt all the way down to her limp toes.

Mary breezed through her cursive penmanship exercises. "I'm finished."

Mr. Gregory glanced up from his book. "Ready for history?" His wire spectacles sat on a bump of a shelf on his nose.

"Yes. You were going to tell me more about war horses in medieval times."

"How do you always smooth talk me into teaching you something about horses? Life is about more than horses, little Miss Mary."

"Horses are everything in history. They are our companions and our transportation. We need their strength for work and their courage to go into battle." She thrust her arm high as if she were carrying a regiment's color banner.

Mr. Gregory put his bony hand up. "Enough, I'm convinced. As I recall, when we left off I was explaining the knight's armor. The knight's body would be completely covered with plates of iron held in place with buckles...."

Mary's eyes fluttered and slipped shut as she tried to imagine the mighty charger and a knight, maybe with a red plume on his helmet, galloping at the enemy. Hot steam blowing from the massive charger's nostrils. "I think my imagination is a little too good, Mr. Gregory. I hear hoof beats."

"Well then, you have whisked me away in your dream, because I hear hoof beats as well."

Mary's eyes flew open. "A horse! It's Papa with my surprise!" She pushed the wheels on her chair as fast as she could down the long dark hallway to the front door. She fumbled with frustration until she managed to spring the heavy wooden door open enough to eek her chair onto the porch. Mary rolled to a stop and oozed a disappointed sigh. It was a horse all right, but it wasn't Papa with a horse for her.

A bay horse pulled a two-wheel buggy down the road. Its black mane and tail rippled in the wind. The horse's knees snapped sharply to its chest, and its hooves flipped debris up from the road. Specks of white foam splattered from the nervous horse's mouth as its head tossed. A girl sat tall and proud on the cushioned seat of the lacquered black buggy. She flicked the buggy whip on the horse's rump when the horse balked going past a flowerbed. As they approached the front of the house, the girl told the horse "whoa".

Joe left his gardening, hurried to the horse's head, and held him still while the girl sprung from the buggy. She nodded to Joe. "I'm here to say hello."

"Very good," he said, smiling. "Will your horse stand tied or should I put him in the barn?" The gelding rubbed his head on Joe's blue plaid shirt, slobbering down the front.

"Treasure's fine here. Thank you." Her black boots wore a new layer of dust, barely dimming the shine. "Hello, I'm Laura," she called as she strode up the stairs. "My family owns the farm next to yours."

"I'm Mary."

"I've seen you sitting by the fence. My parents said I should come over and say 'hello'."

"Yes, I sketch the horses."

Laura perched on the bench swing near Mary, and they stared at each other not sure what to say next.

Mary finally said, "We kinda look alike. You could be my sister."

Laura raised her nose a bit. "I'm twelve. How old are you?"

"I'm twelve too."

"Your hair is longer than mine, but the color's the same." Laura peered into Mary's eyes. "Dark brown. Like mine."

"I'm glad you're here. Since I can't go to school, I've not made any friends."

"I have friends at school. None of them live way out here." Laura gestured over the fields as if she was giving a grand tour.

Mary rearranged her skirt to cover her mismatched socks and leaned toward Laura. "Your horse... is... amazing. His knees tuck all the way up to his chest."

"He's my carriage show horse. We just got home from the Spring Classic, so he's still in his weighted shoes. They help him exaggerate his leg action."

"Do they make his legs hurt?"

"I've wondered about that. Father says he has to wear them if we want to win." Laura pushed with her toes and made the bench swing. One pink and one purple sock peeked over the top of her tall boots.

"If everybody took those heavy shoes off their horses' hooves, they could be judged on their natural action."

"True. But that's not the way life is in the show ring. Come meet him."

Mary avoided the offer. "Maybe we should team up and get the rules changed so they can't use those shoes." She squinted into the sun. "He looks regal, like he could pull the carriage of Princess Anne."

"I love—*love*—to drive him. It's like the wind rushes through me and blasts away all my worries."

"Your life looks pretty perfect from where I'm sitting." Mary's eyes widened with a question. "I have a collection of horse books. Want to see my library?"

"I guess." Laura stood, and Mary rolled the chair past her. "You're crippled?" Laura's hand flew to cover her mouth. "Oh, I'm sorry to be rude. How did I not notice your wheelchair?"

"That's okay. I'm glad you didn't notice at first. Papa says I will walk someday."

"What happened? Were you born like that?"

"No. I got a virus that attacked my muscles when I was four."

"Well, you can't give it to anybody else can you?" Laura took a tiny step backward.

"No. You're safe." Not meaning to, Mary glared at Laura. Nudging open the screen door, she wheeled along the wide hallway to a carved-wooden door with Laura right behind her. Mary paused at the door. "You ready for this?"

Laura shrugged, but smiled politely. The door swung smoothly open, revealing a cozy space with tall wooden bookcases, a carved desk, and one lounge chair covered in soft pink fabric.

"Tada, my horse library."

"Wow." Laura's mouth hung open as she turned to take it all in. "Are they all horse books?"

Mary laughed. "Do girls read other kinds of books?"

"No, I guess not."

Mary lifted a black book from a shelf and placed it before Laura. "This is my most favorite book, *Black Beauty*. I'm related to the author, and I'm even named after her mother. Anna died a few months after it was published. See, it was signed by her mother,

Mary Sewell." Mary pointed to the inscription on the title page. "Did you know Anna Sewell was lame?"

"No. What happened to her?"

"She fell when she was fourteen, and after that, she couldn't walk." Mary gently closed the book. "She couldn't ride, but she drove a carriage until she became bedridden."

Laura extended her hand and traced the picture of the horse on the cover. "I've always wanted to read *Black Beauty*."

"Since you are my new best friend, you can borrow it." Mary reached for her art portfolio.

Laura hugged *Black Beauty* to her chest. "Since you are my new best friend, let me take you on a buggy ride."

The artwork forgotten, Mary grinned. "That's a Cloud 9. Let's go." She stopped short and added, "We'd have to be back before my papa comes home. He thinks everything fun is too dangerous."

"At least he notices."

Treasure's muscles rippled, and his black tail flew as the buggy clattered down the road.

"How long have you had Treasure?"

"He was born at our farm. He's six. He's great fun in the show ring. When he hears the music, he comes alive. If he had fingers, he'd be snapping 'em with the beat." Laura tapped him lightly. "See? Like that. The more the crowd claps for him the higher he lifts his head and knees. He's a born showoff."

"I've never been to a horse show. Maybe my papa can bring me to your next show." Mary clutched the buggy rail as the wheel hit a rut.

"There is another this weekend. You have to come."

"Oooh, I'd love to. I bet you win, don't you?"

"He always comes home with a ribbon." Laura clucked to Treasure. She turned to Mary with mischief in her eyes. "Want to drive?"

"Oh, can I? Anna Sewell drove a team. I can do it. I'm sure I can."

Laura positioned the reins in Mary's hands. "Cluck to make Treasure go forward and say 'whoa' to stop."

Mary said, "Pull on one rein to turn as if his bit of steel was in my own mouth."

"That's right! How'd you know that?" Laura asked.

"My library is the best. I'm reading a book now about riding without a saddle or a bridle." The reins jiggled in her fingers with the trot rhythm.

"No way!"

"The techniques in my book are from Australia, but I've heard the American Indians had secret ways with horses too."

"Australia. We should go there." Laura's eyes widened, and she nodded. "Let's do it."

"If Papa finds a miracle cure there, we'll be on the next boat." Mary laughed.

"Maybe I'll find a miracle cure for you someday. I want to be a doctor."

"You wouldn't have time for horses."

"I'll always have time for horses. I want to compete in Olympic dressage."

"Ladies can't ride in the Olympics." Mary flashed a puzzled look.

"They can now! Lis Hartel with her horse, Jubilee, has been selected for the Denmark Equestrian Olympic Team."

In the distance, a huge white truck rumbled toward them. A dust storm billowed in its wake. Laura snatched the reins from

Mary and drew Treasure to a halt. "What's a truck that big doing on our road?"

"He must be lost."

Laura held the horse firmly. "He must be crazy to go so fast. Can't he see us?"

Treasure stiffened. The horse pulled against the reins and jigged in place.

"Whoa, boy. Whoa," Laura pleaded.

"What are we going to do?" Mary's voice shrilled an octave higher. She scanned the fence lines looking for a gate they could escape through.

The nearby cows lifted their heads to stare. When one cow bolted away, the herd followed with a collective bellow. Treasure twisted in the traces. Laura steadied him. The horse backed into the cart, angling it farther into the middle of the road. Laura snapped the reins sharply on his rump. He shook his head and pushed backward. She popped his rump with the buggy whip, but she may as well have been using a feather duster as much attention as he paid to it.

"We've got to get out of the way!" Mary gripped the side of the buggy with one hand and squeezed Laura's arm with the other.

"We don't have room to turn the rig around. We couldn't outrace a truck, anyway!"

The truck roared toward them. When it hit a rut, it swerved into the grass and almost swiped the fence before bouncing back onto the dirt road.

"We have to do something." Mary jerked on Laura's sleeve.

"You're right. I need to lead him off to the side. Take the reins," Laura yelled as she leaped from the buggy and ran to Treasure's head. Treasure reared with Laura hanging on to his bridle, lifting her high into the air. She tossed about like a rag tied to a clothesline.

Brakes screeched, and smoke poured from under the truck as its wheels locked and it skidded toward them.

Treasure squealed in terror, twisted, and bolted. He dragged Laura off her feet, and she fell to the ground. Mary screamed and sawed on the reins as Treasure lost all reason. He raced headlong toward a small open space between the back of the truck and the fence. The horse could fit, but the buggy would never make it through.

At that moment, the truck veered from the road. It plowed through the fence and bounced into the pasture. An ancient oak tree in its path cracked and split as the truck rammed it. The hood popped up, and steam spewed six feet high. Blue sparks from the engine shot skyward.

Laura rolled over on the road and sat up as she knocked tiny, embedded pebbles from her arm. Treasure streaked away with Mary bobbing in the cart. Mary stopped screaming and commanded "whoa, whoa". She bumped the rein nearest the fence in a steady rhythm. The horse finally dropped out of his gallop into a jerky trot. Where the grassy shoulder of the road widened, she pulled one rein as hard as she could and hauled the runaway rig around.

As they neared Laura, she lunged and grabbed for Treasure's bridle. He snorted and stomped. "Whoa." Laura talked to him as she rubbed his neck. "You're okay now."

Mary's eyes widened at the mangled truck cab. "Think the driver's dead?"

"Should I go look?" Laura didn't sound convinced.

"No, you can't. It might blow up."

"Fire!" Laura pointed to the truck. She ran to the buggy and leapt in before Treasure could run her down again.

The truck door creaked and swung open. A young man fell from the seat and hit the ground. He struggled, hauled himself to his feet, and staggered away from the truck. He hobbled a step and dropped again to the ground.

"He can't walk." Mary gasped as flames shot from under the engine.

Laura snapped the reins, and Treasure popped into a strong trot. "We can't leave him there. It's going to blow up." Laura raced the buggy to him as he hauled himself to his feet again. "Get in quick," she yelled.

Mary tugged on his arm and held tight to the man's shirt.

With him dangling from the buggy with one leg up over the side, they bounced across the rough pasture. "Go. Get us out of here!"

At the road, Laura slowed the horse. The man dropped from the buggy and clung to a fence board. "My gas pedal stuck. I couldn't stop."

A car slid to a stop. Laura's neighbor jumped out with a red fire extinguisher and yelled at the girls. "Get away from here—now!" He ran past the truck driver and plastered white foam across the engine. Laura cued Treasure, and he exploded into a power trot.

After putting the disaster far behind them, Laura drew the horse to an abrupt halt. "So scary."

"You're shaking." Mary wrapped her arms around Laura, and they clung to each other.

"That was as bad as my dream."

"You dreamed a truck would hit us?"

"No, it's not like that. I dream I'm riding a huge, red, raging horse, and I fall off into an abyss," said Laura.

"What's an abyss?"

"It's a horrible place. It's where the devil waits." Laura shivered and rubbed goose bumps off her arms. "The horse won't stop. It runs like it's insane. It jumps off a ledge to nowhere, and I fall toward rocky spikes. I'm screaming and I wake up."

"If I had a dream like that, I'd move out of my head." Mary echoed a shiver. "Want me to pray for you? Mrs. Tate prays for me all the time, so I know how to do it."

"I guess, but I don't see how it can help."

"Let's try it." Mary brought her hands together, closed her eyes, and bowed her head.

Laura dropped her chin and rested her shoulder against Mary as she prayed.

"God? Please protect Laura from her bad dream. Amen."

"That's it?"

"He's busy. If I keep it short, I'm sure he's still listening when I'm done. Now, you need to pray the same thing every night before you go to sleep."

Laura looked over at Mary, but didn't say what she was obviously thinking—it would never work. She turned her glazed-over eyes back to the road and sat there as though she couldn't muster the strength to drive on. Then she broke the stillness with a huge, lip-fluttering sigh.

Mary answered with a sputtering sigh of her own. "If my papa finds out what happened... When you tell your parents, please don't make it too big of a deal."

"Why tell them at all?" Laura lifted the reins and cued Treasure to walk on.

"Because it's the right thing. Besides the neighbor saw us."

"I could say a truck scared Treasure, but we handled it."

"Yes. That's perfect. It's even the truth," Mary agreed. "If my papa knew what really happened, he would slap me into a nice, safe boarding school with a nun rapping my knuckles."

"My parents would say 'that's nice, dear' if they even noticed I was talking." Laura clucked to Treasure, and the horse perked into a flashy trot.

"Papa can't find out." Mary stuck out her bottom lip and frowned.

19

When they trotted up the road to the house, Mary's eyes locked onto her papa waiting on the porch. "Uh-oh. I hope he's not angry" As she waved to him, she said "look happy" under her breath. "He never lets me do anything fun. And slightly dangerous—like sledding, forget about it." Lifting her voice, she shouted, "Look at me, Papa! Isn't this the best ever?" She flashed her biggest, happiest smile.

As he lifted her from the buggy, she introduced him to Laura. He looked Laura and her rig up and down and smiled. "Very glad you came to see Mary. Not many girls out here."

Still traumatized from the truck scare, Laura managed a shy smile.

"You come again, anytime." He turned and carried Mary to the house.

"Thank you, Laura." Mary peered over his shoulder. She held a finger in front of her pursed lips in a silent "shh" reminding Laura to keep their secret. "Come again soon," she called.

"You look a little flushed. Is everything all right? I think the buggy ride might have been too much for you?"

"It was an adventure I will never forget. I had *so* much fun! Laura's a great driver."

Papa whispered in Mary's ear. "Do you want to see your surprise?"

"Oh yes!"

"Close your eyes." He carried her into her library. "Open."

On the bookshelf sat a pair of crystal horse heads with pink color swirled in the solid glass. Not quite what she had hoped for, but she knew someday it would be a real horse—for sure. "Pink horse bookends. I've never seen anything so fine." She laid her head on his shoulder.

"Always the best for you, my Mary. All the way from Venice, Italy." He squeezed her. "My trip to Florida was everything I hoped it would be. I think the treatment is a good possibility, and I want to get you started as soon as possible." He settled her in the chair. "How's that sound? We leave on Saturday."

"So soon? Please, no, Papa." She moved her chair back away from him. "I finally make a friend, and I have to leave?" Her hands poised on the wheels, ready to make her chair fly away.

"It's all arranged."

"Laura invited me to come watch her at the horse show."

"I know you'd love that, but it has to be another time. We're going to Florida."

Her hands flopped into her lap. "None of the therapies work, Papa." Her chin sank to her chest. "Please don't make me go right now."

CHAPTER THREE

*M*orning rain showers ruined Mary's plans to sketch the foals, so she curled on the porch swing with a horse book. Papa came outside and settled beside her. She looked past him into the drizzle.

"The weather will clear up after lunch. I've asked Joe to move a chair under the tree, so you will be able to sketch later and not sit in the wet grass. Mr. Gregory's not feeling well today and isn't coming for your school lessons."

Her eyes brightened. "We can spend the day together. We could go to the soda shop."

"Not today. I have too much to do before we leave for Florida."

Her face slumped. "Papa!" Mary blinked a tear away. "I could go with you?"

He stood and buttoned his camel-colored, tailored vest. "Not this time. Perhaps your new friend can come again. I don't want you going out in her buggy though. Anything could happen. You're much too delicate to be flung about in a carriage."

"But…"

"Those are my rules. I'll see you at dinner." He kissed her cheek and wiped away a tear with his finger. "No tears. We don't always get what we want in life, and we don't cry about it." Tenting a newspaper over his neat brown hair, he leaned into the rain and dashed to the car.

Her disappointment raced after him. "Come back, Papa. Please listen…" She stared after the car long after it disappeared.

When the sun popped out, her heart still gripped the gloom, so she went looking for comfort in her library. Soon she transformed into the book character who could run and ride. At her command waited a white mare. She would weave flowers and ribbons in the pony's thick, silky mane. People spoke of them with awe. They were loved and known far and wide for the gift-wrapped books they delivered to children on remote homesteads.

A clip-clop rhythm returned Mary to reality. "Laura!" She shut her book and placed it on the shelf.

As Mary reached the porch, Laura halted Treasure by the hitching rail. Waving at Mary, she snapped a line to his necktie strap and wrapped it a few times around the cedar railing. Laura peered about to make sure no one would overhear them. "How'd it go with your papa?"

"He never suspected a thing. And yours?"

"My story didn't impress them at all. I could have been telling them about the weather. It's easy to put stuff over on them when they don't pay much attention." Laura smiled, but her eyes looked sad.

"You don't mean that."

"Yes. Yes, I do. My father is always gone on business. Mother checks the barns first thing every morning. She rides, but not with me. She says she has to concentrate on her equitation. Like she needs another blue ribbon." Laura puckered as if she had a mouth of lemon juice and crossed her eyes. "After that, she's gone. She does lunch with the society ladies or volunteers in the hospital. You get the idea."

"She sounds important."

"Oh, she is. So important. She only remembers me because she needs me to show in the juvenile classes."

"I'm sure it's not like that. At least you have a mother."

"Not really. You brave enough to ride along while I exercise Treasure?" Laura asked.

"Didn't he get enough exercise yesterday?"

"Yes! But I couldn't exactly tell the trainer that."

"I guess not." Mary pointed to the swing. "Papa said I couldn't. Can you sit with me for a while?"

"Our parents are the exact opposite." Laura plopped onto the swing. "Your papa controls everything, and mine ignores me." One baby blue and one outrageous blue sock edged over Laura's boot tops. "I have to get things ready for the show this Saturday. Did you ask your papa if he would bring you?"

"He's taking me to Florida, for another therapy that won't work."

Laura pumped her fist. "Never give up! Your papa's not giving up."

"There's no use. I've been to all kinds of crazy places, and the things I've had to try are too stupid. Like putting hot rocks on my back."

"That does sound a little crazy." Laura grimaced.

"He treats me like I'm going to break. I can't talk him out of anything he's set his mind on. And he thinks *I* have a stubborn streak." Mary frowned. "Let's go inside. I want to show you my sketches of your foals."

"I'd love to see your art. I wish I could draw. The horses I draw look like belching sea dragons."

"Come on." Mary rolled into the library and spread her sketches across her school desk.

Laura leafed through them. "These are good—really, really good."

"The foals are my favorite."

"I could show your art to my father. I bet he would put a few sketches in our sale catalog."

"How can you sell the babies?"

"It's the way it is. I've gotten used to it. I fall in love with each new foal crop every spring."

Mary slipped the ribbon off a separate stack of sketches and fanned them out. "Look at these. Don't you think this is the sweetest baby of them all? I've named her Illusion because she is so much more than a pretty, red bay."

"You're not going to believe this—what a quirk." Laura's fingers tapped her chest. "I was there when she was born. After she got past the wobbly leg stage, she walked pressed against her dam. She looked like a mirrored reflection or an illusion. I named her Life's Illusion." Laura bent over the sketches, picking out one of the filly with her dam's tail cascading across the foal's face.

"We've named her the same thing? That's a sign, don't you think?"

"If you say so. She has a nice face, and her conformation's good. She isn't a little dolly like the dappled gray. Even though she's not my favorite, it's still a shame about her leg." Laura shook her head and frowned. "I used to show her dam. After she won High Point Champion, she was more valuable as a—"

"What do you mean, 'it's a shame about her leg'?" Mary scrunched her forehead as she leaned into Laura's face.

"Poor thing was born with a club foot. The barn manager decided to watch her for a few months to see if it would correct itself, but it's not looking good."

"I noticed she limped sometimes. I didn't see anything wrong with her legs."

"The veterinarian told us the misalignment of her hoof was the reason for her lameness."

In her own head, Mary sprang to her feet. "What will you do to help her?"

"There is nothing to be done. She will be put down when the vet comes for his next scheduled visit."

"You're going to kill her?"

"Not me! I don't have any say in it."

"How can you let that happen?" Mary sat ramrod straight.

Laura tapped the toe of her boot on the table leg. "You don't know anything about managing a horse farm. You can't learn that from books." She dropped the sketches onto the table. "My father told me to stay out of the business. He said it was the barn manager's decision, and he knows what's best."

"I'll buy her. I'll ask Papa for money, and I'll buy her."

"You can't. They won't sell her, because Father said she would reflect badly on the farm's breeding program and ruin our reputation."

"Killing her would be worse for your reputation."

Laura put her hands on her hips. "This is not my fault! And there's nothing I can do about it. If that's the way you're going to be, I'm leaving now and never coming here again."

As Laura twisted away, Mary reached out and caught her new friend by the sleeve. "Wait. I'm so sorry." Her fingers clung to Laura's riding coat. "Maybe we can come up with something."

"I told you, there isn't anything I can do." Laura tugged her sleeve from Mary's grasp.

"Weren't you just telling me to never give up?" Mary swung her arm to mimic Laura's earlier gesture. "You can't give up on Illusion.

27

We both named her the same thing! We should work together to save her. Can you take me to talk to your barn manager?"

"Won't your papa be mad?"

"Only if he finds out. I have to do this."

Mary looked everywhere at once as Laura drove up to a red barn with a black metal horse mounted over the door. "Your farm looks like Lexington Equine Park! It's all so beautiful—like a painting."

"My father says buyers expect it. Will you be okay alone with Treasure while I go find Mr. Todd? I could tie him to the rail."

"After yesterday, there's nothing he can do to scare me. No problem."

"That wasn't his fault. I'll hurry."

In a few minutes, Laura returned. "He's coming."

Mr. Todd strode out of the barn. His straight, white teeth gleamed. Mary hadn't pictured him with a pleasant smile.

"I thought he'd look evil."

Laura flashed a puzzled look and shook her head. "Mr. Todd is great. He loves the horses. He gets up in the middle of the night with the mares when they foal. He bottle-fed one orphan colt for two months. In the first week, that's every two hours."

"But he can get rid of a foal because it's lame."

"It's not like he wants to. He says he has to do what's right." Laura quickly glanced at Mr. Todd and whispered to Mary. "Shh, he'll hear you."

"Hello, young lady. It's nice to see another girl Laura's age in the area. Laura said you have some questions about the foals."

"Yes, sir. Thank you. I wanted to ask you about the little red bay filly, Illusion. What can be done for her leg?"

"She's a sad case. What needs to be done is not worth doing. She needs an expensive surgery, and there's no guarantee of the results."

"Isn't her life worth as much as any other?"

He stuck one foot in the wheel spokes and leaned on the buggy rail. "She'd likely never walk normally. If she were in the wild, she would be the first foal picked off by the wolves."

"She's not in the wild." Mary shook her head at him. Why didn't he get that?

"No, but nature sometimes knows best. We could never sell or show her. We couldn't breed her and chance having foals with leg deformities. There's nothing to be done, I'm afraid."

"Isn't it okay for her to live even if she's not perfect? I think she deserves a chance."

He stepped away from the cart. Removing his cap, he combed his fingers through his hair and snapped it back onto his head. "As I said, it's expensive. Even if she survived the surgery, the recovery is long and complicated."

"But it might work?"

"For one thing, we don't have the manpower to devote to one horse that will likely never amount to anything. It doesn't make financial sense for the farm. I've been raising foals a long time and in my experience, the surgery probably wouldn't work. I know that's not what you want to hear. I have to make hard decisions sometimes." He touched his cap and tipped his head to the girls. "I understand your concern. It wasn't an easy decision for me. Now I have work to do. Nice visiting with you, ladies."

As he walked away, Mary made a grumpy face to his back. "It's not right. He can't have Illusion killed. We can squeeze her through the fence, and she can hide on our farm."

"Keep thinkin'. That plan won't work."

"I have to convince my papa to buy her, and you have to convince your father to sell her. Deal?"

Laura shook her head. "I'm telling you, it'll never work. I know my father. He won't budge."

Mary intertwined all her fingers and rubbed the heels of her hands together until they burned red. She had to be careful to tell her papa about the filly without revealing she had ridden in Laura's buggy.

Mrs. Tate pressed the door open. "Want to come inside, dear, before the mosquitoes find you?"

"No, thank you. I have to talk to Papa, and he should be home soon."

"I'm keeping your dinner in the oven. Oh, he's turning onto the farm road now."

As he walked to the porch, Mary smiled big. "I love you, Papa."

"That's nice to hear." He kissed the top of her head and sat across from her. "You look like you are about to explode with exciting news, so let it out."

"Laura came today. We talked about the red bay filly. They named her Illusion too. Don't you think that's from God?"

"Not sure what you mean, but it's certainly a coincidence."

"Mrs. Tate calls things like that a God-incidence."

"Is that what has you all excited?"

"Yes, I think God wants us to buy Illusion."

Papa scratched his head and pondered the reality sitting before him. "I know you love watching and sketching the foals, but it is quite another thing to own one. Horses are not kittens or puppies."

"So she would never be able to sit in my lap. She could still be my best friend. I think she was meant for me. You know I already love her."

"As do I, but she has a happy home, and we get all the benefits of enjoying her without the expense. Not to mention the trouble." Papa patted her on the knee. "We better go in to dinner." He held open the door for Mary, but she didn't budge.

"That's just it, Papa! She doesn't have a happy home at all." Her voice grew shrill. "They are going to murder her."

"What?"

"Laura said Illusion was born with a crooked leg. They can't use her as a broodmare, and she doesn't have enough flash to show her. When the vet comes again, he is going to put her down! Please, Papa, we have to do something. We can't let them kill her." She reached out, grabbed his shirt, and gave it a little tug.

"They are knowledgeable horse people. They must be doing the best thing for everyone."

"They act like she is worthless. You don't want her because she's lame. I'm lame too, in case you haven't noticed. Should something be allowed to live only if it's perfect? Do you think I should be killed?"

"Mary, that is absurd." With one finger, he pointed into the house, telling her to go ahead of him.

Mary still didn't budge. "They could fix her!" she pleaded. "There's a surgery."

Papa took in a deep breath, but she didn't let him squeeze a word in. "It costs money," she said. "And that won't..."

He raised his hand and stopped her right there. "The farm has to consider the cost."

"Does a crooked leg make her worthless? Am I worth the same as her—nothing?"

"You are out of bounds, young lady."

"Is she too much trouble? Am I too much trouble too?"

Papa inclined toward her and pointed his finger in her face. "I've never in twelve years spanked you, but I'm about to if you say one more word."

Mary wheeled her chair past Papa, who still held the door open, nearly squashing his toes. She rolled down the hall toward her bedroom as fast as she could.

An hour later, Papa found her face down on her bed where she had flung herself. Tears wet her soft pink pillow. "You should come have some dinner." He slid his hand onto her shoulder. "I'll think about it while we are gone. Maybe—only maybe—I might go talk to Laura's parents when we come home from Florida."

"She'll be dead by then." Mary's eyes felt puffy. "You have to go now, before it's too late for Illusion. I'm begging you, Papa. Before it's too late for me."

CHAPTER FOUR

A long black car waited outside the house early the next morning.

"I can't leave." Mary's arms locked across her chest.

"Yes, you have to. I tried to catch them before they left for the horse show. There is nothing more we can do right now."

"We could go to the horse show."

"We have an appointment that was difficult to arrange with a well-respected, prominent physician. We are going." Papa cradled Mary and carried her to the car as she wept on his shoulder. "Your healing is my overriding concern."

Mary raised her head to look him in the eye. "If she dies..."

"Tell you what, after we arrive in Florida, I could call and talk to Laura's father. They should be home from the show by then."

Mary sniffled and wiped her nose. "Oh, Papa, would you really? You're the best."

"Don't get your hopes up. Since the farm manager thinks treatment for the foal isn't likely to help, I don't want to throw money away on it. They know more about these things than we do. I'm afraid I could spend a fortune and the horse would never be anything more than a pasture ornament—at best." He slid her onto the back seat of the car and leaned to look directly into her eyes. "Have you considered you could put the horse through all sorts of treatments and surgery, and it might stay lame and be in tremendous pain?"

Mary covered her ears with her hands and shook her head.

"You promised, Papa! You promised you would call about Illusion when we got here."

"It is considered rude to call people before the sun comes up. It will have to wait until we get back to the hotel tonight."

Papa carried her across the beach toward two white tents near the shoreline. The roar of the ocean and the screech of a seagull greeted them. In the distance, a flock of pelicans flew in a *V* formation toward the morning sun.

"The water, Papa! It's the color of emeralds."

"It is indeed. The sand on this coast is quartz that washed down from the Appalachian Mountains."

"If any water can cure me, this is it."

"This is a special place. Some say it is a place of miracles."

Mary whispered into Papa's ear. "He doesn't look like a doctor today. Shorts and a floppy hat?"

"What do you expect the man to wear on the beach? A white coat?" He shifted her in his arms.

"That would be funny."

Papa greeted the clinic doctor. "Thank you for arranging all this for my Mary."

Dr. Krane placed his reading glasses on his medical journal and rose from his beach chair in the tent's shade. "Glad you found the right beach. I've been looking forward to getting started on your therapy, Mary. Clinically, I've every reason to believe this treatment will restore you to health." He gestured to a tanned young woman in a bathing suit and shorts. "Evelyn will be with you in the tidal pool."

Mary frowned at the chair apparatus placed in the ocean a few yards from shore. The white tent awning fluttered in the quiet breeze. "You're putting me way out there? I can't swim!"

"You will wear a life jacket, and it's safe, I assure you," Dr. Krane said.

Her fingers clamped onto the fabric of Papa's shirt. She didn't feel at all assured.

Papa walked in step with the doctor to the shoreline.

"We utilize the physical properties of water buoyancy and resistance. The buoyancy reduces stress and counteracts gravity while the resistance allows for strengthening the muscles you need to walk again." The doctor patted her knee.

Papa waded out into the water and eased her into the therapy chair.

Evelyn got right to work. "Tense and tighten both legs as much as you can and hold it to the count of three. Let's do five repetitions."

Mary swirled her hands in the cool water, trying to catch bubbles in the surf. "I feel light enough to float."

"Yes, saltwater gives you a lift." Evelyn kneaded, stretched, and pulled each muscle group. "Feel this sand." She reached under the water and lifted a handful of sand and poured the creamy granules into Mary's hand.

"Like soft powder."

Evelyn nodded as she grasped an ankle and supported Mary's knee, moving it as if to pedal a bicycle. A rush of water cascaded over Mary, dragging along a piece of seaweed with a tiny crab clinging to the plant.

Mary scooped up the seaweed. "I can almost see through this crab. He's very cute."

"Many people keep them in aquariums to clean the tank."

"Not my kind of pet. I'm going to train horses someday."

Evelyn switched sides on Mary. "I'm glad you have high expectations for the therapy." Evelyn bicycled Mary's other leg.

Mary clenched her fists as she tightened her leg muscles. "It's got to work. A foal at home needs me. She could die if I don't come up with something—soon."

"I'm sorry. I know what they do to your heart."

"My papa says my mama took me for rides...." Her voice softened as the waves curled and rolled to the shore. "I wish I could remember it."

"My father worked as a groom at a racehorse ranch. Those young racehorses were always hurting themselves. I got to ride them to the beach and swim them in the ocean." She grasped Mary's heels in the palms of her hands and pedaled. "To think a twelve-hundred-pound free spirit would allow me to ride on its back." Evelyn stopped to consider it. "Everything is more beautiful viewed between the ears of a horse." A wistful look flushed her face. "My dream is to work with horses."

"That's my dream too. I want to believe it could happen for me. But it gets so discouraging to try to walk, and I can't. Evelyn, my legs are getting tired."

"That means the muscles are trying. Dr. Krane will want to take you to the Ponce DeLeon pool tomorrow."

Mary peeked across the beach at Papa, stretched out nearby in a lounge chair, basking in the sun. "Papa said it's the 'Fountain Of Youth', so why do I need that?"

"There is something mystical, magical, special about the water. You wait. It is like no pool you have ever been in."

"If it's good for me..." Mary's voice trailed off. "Then Illusion needs it too."

The hotel desk clerk handed Papa a note with their room kcy. He read it and handed it to Mary. "It's me—Laura. Call me NOW. I have to talk to you NOW." She crumpled the note in her hands. "Papa, something's wrong. We have to call."

"I can see that," he said.

Mary's fingers fidgeted with the note as Papa placed the call and handed the phone to Mary. "Is Laura there?" She looked anxiously at Papa. "Did she leave me a message? This is Mary." Her eyes caught Papa's, and she shook her head no. "Did she say anything about Illusion? When will she be home?" Mary listened and handed the phone back to Papa. "We just missed them. The family went to visit her Aunt Claire. The housekeeper thinks they will be home in a few days. Why would Laura leave Illusion, unless they already put her down?"

Mary's first words the next morning were "Papa, please try to call the farm manager. I have to know what's going on."

Papa glanced at his watch. He dialed, and they listened to the phone ring and ring some more at Laura's house. Mary clamped onto his arm as he tried to hang up. "Please let it ring until someone, anyone answers. Somebody has to be there."

"We are due at the spring soon. It's likely the housekeeper got a few days off since the family is away, so it's not much use calling an empty house. We are going to have to sort this out when we can get home."

Following Dr. Krane and Evelyn, Papa carried Mary down a narrow path through the woods. An owl glided to a branch overhead and hooted as if perturbed to be awakened. Red birds and wrens flitted and chirped. The place radiated a mix of busyness and complete peace.

Mary pulled a strand of Spanish moss from a branch. "I thought the water would be the same as at the beach, but it's clear instead of that pretty green."

Papa nodded. "I have every hope this place will do wonders for you." He shifted her weight. "Aw, my sweet Mary, you are getting heavy. I wish I'd let Evelyn take you on her fancy, big-wheeled cart."

Mary rested her head on his shoulder and didn't speak.

Several steps later, he asked, "Where did you go just now?"

"I was praying about Illusion and me. A mighty God can heal us both."

"He's not a vending machine. Put in a prayer and out pops a blessing." Papa shifted her weight. "If it worked that way, your mama would be with ... Sometimes we have to let go of what we hold dear."

"Mrs. Tate said God doesn't give us everything we ask for, but he has a good reason."

"She is a wise woman. We can't understand many things this side of heaven."

"I wish you'd tell me more about Mama."

"And you have a right to know, but it's still so hard, even after all these years, to talk about her."

"Is Mama in heaven?"

"Any other alternative is infinitely more painful to consider."

"Like there is no heaven?"

Dr. Krane turned to check on them. Mary waved. He and Evelyn disappeared down the trail. Papa eased Mary onto a smooth rock bench along the path and sat beside her. "She believed there is a heaven." His eyes scanned the sky. "I would sit by her bed and hold her hand. She would gaze at something behind me and seemed to be listening to someone I couldn't see. Her face looked radiant, even joyful. On that last day, I held her in my arms as I felt her spirit leave her body quietly behind. Yes, I believe your mama is in heaven." He leaned forward with his elbows on his legs, bowed his head, and studied the dirt under his feet.

Mary reached out and rested her hand on his arm. Was that dark spot in the dirt a tear?

The birds chirped and flitted about. The sun filtered through the treetops, casting shadows across the path. Life went on around them.

"If they put Illusion to sleep, will she go to heaven? Would she be with Mama?"

He turned his head to look at her and then back down to the dirt. With a sigh, he said, "Now, you are taxing my theological understanding as well as my patience. How did we get on such heavy topics?"

"Because I can't stop thinking." She pressed against him. "Would you call the farm again, please? If we could only talk to Mr. Todd. I'm sure he knows what's wrong. I can't stop thinking about what they might be doing to Illusion while I'm here bathing in magical pools praying for a miracle."

39

Evelyn helped Mary into the pool and supported her as she floated in the clear spring. "Come in the water too, Papa," Mary called. "It feels amazing. It's silky."

Papa stopped talking to Dr. Krane. "Maybe tomorrow. Relax and soak." He slumped on a nearby bench. He tilted his chin upward and sideways, popping and stretching his neck.

As she fingered the ferns along the bank, Mary thought she had never seen him look so tired and discouraged.

Evelyn eased her to sit on a submerged, flat rock next to a cypress tree, disturbing the privacy of an iridescent skink. It darted sideways around the tree. Warm water covered Mary's shoulders. Reaching to pool bottom, Evelyn lifted a piece of light green algae from the sandy floor and handed it to Mary.

"It feels feather soft. It tickles even. What an interesting place. I can see why people come here."

"Billions of gallons of mineral-rich water flow from this spring every day. You'll feel different when you get out. Your skin will be silky soft, and maybe you'll notice other changes too."

"I'd like it to be different, but my life is in a wheelchair, and that's just how it is. Except now, it's about Illusion too." Mary skimmed her fingers on the water's surface in the reflection of the weeping willow. "If it's not already too late. Such a beautiful, sweet foal. How could they...?"

Evelyn splashed a water bug away without commenting. She shifted behind Mary. "Do your best to kick your feet."

Mary drifted lightly, her body supported by Evelyn. "Nothing's happening."

"That's okay. Don't expect too much at first. Let your legs relax completely and drift to the bottom. The life jacket will hold you, and I want you to put your feet on the sand and see if you can push up."

As Mary squished her toes in the spring's sand floor, tiny air bubbles burst through. "I think my toes can wiggle better or maybe I just want it so much." The sand puffed like powdered sugar under her feet. "I feel my leg muscles! I'm so light in the water my legs are sorta holding me up. They're holding me up, Papa!" Mary screeched. "My legs. My legs are trying to work!"

His head snapped up. Eyes wide, he sprang from his seat. Dr. Krane jumped to his feet. Papa raced to the water's edge and, without pulling off even his shirt, leapt into the spring water. He plowed through, splashing spray everywhere as he scrambled to her. "Really, Mary? Your muscles are working?" He snatched her up and squeezed. "The miracle I've waited for!" he bellowed as he twirled her around and around.

"You're making me dizzy!" Mary laughed, holding tight to his neck. "It's working!"

He bounced her up and down in the water, making waves in the quiet spring. When he finally stilled, he held her tight. "I'm so grateful." A hush occupied the space around them.

A small school of black fish darted about as he floated her to the bank. She fluttered her fingers to lure them. "I feel my dreams starting to come true. I'm going to ride."

"Wouldn't that be amazing? But give it time," Evelyn cautioned.

The soft water glided off Mary's skin as Papa lifted her from the spring. "My skin feels tingly. Look, the drops of water slide off in a sheet. I don't feel wet at all, and I'm warm all over. This is what Illusion needs."

"That would be a sight. A horse in the spring." Evelyn shook her head. "But people do bring horses to the ocean beach for water therapy from all around."

"Papa, did you hear that? People bring their horses to this amazing water for healing. Wouldn't that be fun?"

"Not from Texas they don't."

CHAPTER FIVE

The days flashed and dragged at the same time. After many hours at the beach and the spring, Mary reserved the evenings for worrying about Illusion. The constant rereading of Laura's note kept Mary on the edge of panic. On the long trip home, Papa went over the exercise treatment plan Mary must continue on her own. She tried to listen, but couldn't concentrate.

The sleek black car rumbled when they turned into the farm driveway. "I'm glad to be home. I've missed Illusion so much." Mary searched the herd of horses for her. "I see her dam. Where is she?" She couldn't breathe.

Papa peered out the window. "She wouldn't be too far from her mother."

"She's gone! I don't see her anywhere. Illusion's mother is there by the oak tree. Look how far away she is from the other mares. Something is wrong." She started shaking.

He reached for her hand. "Don't panic. The foal's out there somewhere. She's probably hiding behind a tree."

"She's not there! All the other foals are there, but Illusion's gone. I knew it. I'll never see her again, and I didn't even get to say goodbye."

Papa carried her to the porch and helped the driver bring their bags to the house. She stared at the pasture. Her body sat rigid even as tears drenched her face. She glared at Papa when he passed.

"I know what you're thinking, but you shouldn't assume the worst. Doesn't everything usually work out better than you could ever imagine?" His eyes searched for agreement in hers.

"I can't stand not knowing. I'm sure they decided there was no hope for Illusion. If only I could have talked to them before they…"

"Let me pay the limo driver, and I'll bring our car around and take you to the horse farm."

As they drove onto the Morgan horse farm, Mary peered out the window. Laura came running to meet the car. "Mary, you're home already."

"Is she dead?"

"I wanted to be there when you got home so I could tell you myself."

"She's dead," Mary wailed. "I knew it."

Laura touched Mary's arm. "She's fine."

"I knew it was too late. It's just too horrible." Mary's voice cracked as her throat tightened. She snapped her chin up to look at Laura. "You said she's fine? You mean it?"

"We tried to call you back, but you'd checked out of the hotel by the time we got home from my Aunt Claire's."

"How'd you do it? You are amazing!"

"I begged my father to give her to me, to us. Come see her for yourself."

Papa lifted Mary from the car, placed her in the wheelchair, and went to the main house. Laura pushed the chair to the barn.

Mary twisted in the seat to see Laura. "He was set against it. The message you left at the hotel—I was sure she was dead. How did you convince him?"

"I'm sorry I scared you. I had great news, not bad. I made a lot of promises to Father, but I'm wondering if my mother might have talked to him about it. He kept looking over at her while we talked, but she never said a word. He was almost too easy to convince." Laura pushed faster. "He won't pay for the surgery, but he said if we raise the money we can do it. He told Mr. Todd to prepare the oversized foaling stall with the thick mats. She's in it now, and he took special care of her while I was gone."

"You are my most clever friend."

Out of breath, Laura dragged open the heavy wooden door to the stall and gave a grand gesture toward Illusion. "There she is."

Mary rolled her chair into the doorway. Illusion cocked her head, stepped forward, and sniffed the chair. Sucking back, the filly snorted. Mary reached toward the foal and cooed. "Hello there. You know me." Illusion tipped her head and flicked her ears. "I'm so relieved to see you. I was afraid I'd lost you forever." Her fingertips stroked the velvety plush muzzle. The filly leaned into Mary's touch. Her fingers rested on the side of Illusion's face, rubbing in little circles. "I'm gonna fight for you with everything I've got." The foal moved her nose in front of Mary's nose and sniffed softly.

Mary blew air back at the filly. "You like me. She likes me!" Mary smiled at Laura and pushed her fingers deeper into the filly's coat. "Why did you wean her? Wouldn't it have been better to keep her mother with her?"

"It's time to wean all the foals. They're old enough now to eat grass and grain."

Illusion rolled back her upper lip, and the girls laughed out loud.

Laura continued, "Mr. Todd has a transport company coming first thing in the morning to take all the broodmares to their summer pasture at our other farm in Navasota. I wanted to make it as easy on Illusion as I could, so I got special permission to wean her first." Laura slipped behind the foal and scratched her little rump at the base of her tail. "Illusion followed her mama into the stall. Then I distracted the foal with some carrot horse cookies in the feeder, so I could slip her dam out. I tied the mare outside the stall. Every hour or so, I moved her a little farther away. Illusion took it like a trooper. Treasure is acting like her big dopey brother. He nickers to her whenever she calls for her mother."

"Couldn't you keep her with another foal?"

"She needs to be kept quiet, and a playmate would want to roughhouse. She's got Treasure nearby, and he adores her. Mother said I don't have to take him to any shows until Illusion can be turned out with the other foals again. Father wasn't happy about it at first. But Mother told him she has another horse she wants me to show this season, so it worked out."

"It does sound like your mother's on our side. Thank you for giving up showing Treasure to help Illusion. You're the best friend." Mary's voice quivered.

"There is one thing I haven't told you... and it's bad."

Mary held her breath.

"My father gave her to us with a big catch. He said this goes against his better judgment. But he'll give her another six weeks. If she doesn't get better or we can't raise the money for the surgery, then he'll have her put down."

"Six weeks!" A boulder rolled onto Mary's chest. "I don't have any money. Do you?"

"Not enough to matter. I talked to the vet." Laura blew a big puff of air from her mouth. "And you don't want to know."

Mary sighed, "My papa said this whole thing was a crazy scheme. What are we gonna do?"

"I don't know." Laura shrugged and combed her fingers through Illusion's fluffy tail. "I thought you might've been working on a few ideas while you were gone."

"Well, I haven't come up with anything—yet."

CHAPTER SIX

$\mathcal{P}$each juice dripped from Mary's fingers as the fuzzy skin dropped into a bowl. Mrs. Tate skimmed the piecrust skillfully from the wooden board and into the pie pan.

Mary asked, "Have you seen my Morgan mare carving? The one that was my mama's."

"No. You had it in the library right after it broke, but I haven't seen it since. I'm sorry I didn't have any ideas on fixing it. I know how special that horse is to you and I'll keep an eye out for it. It has to be around here somewhere."

"So strange. Papa must have taken it. But, if he found it, he would've been angry with me, and he would've said something." She laid down the paring knife she'd used to skin peaches. "It's a mystery," she said, wiping peach drips on a towel. "Mrs. Tate? If you needed a lotta *lotta* money fast, how would you get it?"

"Ask for a loan, I guess." Mrs. Tate slid chopped fruit into a bowl.

Mary pilfered a slice. "Would you give me a loan?"

Mrs. Tate tilted her full chin down and looked over her glasses at Mary as she tossed peaches in sugar. "Is this about that horse? Not a chance."

Mary grinned and snagged another peach piece before it slipped into the crust.

"Oh, of course, it is."

"If a loan is out, what do you think about my selling homemade cookies?"

Mrs. Tate smirked. "You'd have to sell a lot of cookies."

"I could set up a booth and sell them at the fair next week."

"And who are you expecting will bake all these cookies for you? Pray tell?"

"I will! I have to." Mary tilted her head and turned on the charm. "You're the best cookie baker ever. If you help me, the cookies will sell in a blink."

Mrs. Tate rolled her eyes and slid the pie into a hot oven. "I see Miss Laura coming down the road. She has a new horse pulling her buggy today."

"Treasure is busy being a big brother." Mary spun her chair and headed to the porch to watch them power trot up the road. The horse's front hooves flicked as if a performer was waving to an adoring crowd.

"I brought someone to meet you," Laura called as she halted the white mare. The horse lowered her regal head and tilted one curved ear back toward Laura.

"She's a beauty. Her mane is gorgeous, and her tail almost drags on the ground."

"She won Best Of Show four years in a row in her younger days. Her name is Crown Jewel. My mother used to show her in equitation and pleasure driving classes." Laura jumped from the buggy.

"Mr. Todd decided to give her a year off from raising a foal. I've been riding her to make sure she's not forgotten her manners and she'll be perfect for you."

"For me? What are you doing?" Mary gawked as Laura unhooked Jewel from the buggy.

"I have another surprise for you. I didn't get to tell you last night since all we talked about was Illusion."

Mary bubbled with smiles. "I love good surprises."

"While you were gone, I went to the Hunt Library. It's downstairs in the same building as my school. Miss Dann, she's the librarian, loves horses too." Laura reached out and touched Mary as she shared her brilliant idea. "You should meet her. She helped me research your new miracle cure. Tell me where this is crazy—okay?" Laura spread her fingers, held her hands high, and her body swayed with emphasis. "Muscles need to move to get stronger. If you can't walk, it's hard to strengthen them—am I right?"

Mary nodded.

Laura smiled and giggled. "Anyway, Miss Dann found an article in a horse magazine from The Netherlands about therapeutic riding. Wouldn't that just be perfect for you? I rode Jewel in the round pen with my eyes closed to experiment. I listened to my body. Muscles all over tightened and relaxed to keep me balanced."

"How clever! I so love it."

"I dug an old Western saddle we used to start colts out of a storeroom, and Mr. Joe put on straps to hold you in the saddle."

"I'm so flipped." Mary's mouth drooped open.

"At dinner last night, my father said your papa was leaving town, so I knew we would be in the clear to try it out today. Mr. Joe told me he would help us." Laura looked around and lowered her voice.

"Your papa said no buggy rides. He never said anything about riding in a saddle."

"And I thought I was sneaky and devious. You're a great friend for me. I could learn things from you."

"You're calling me bad names. I thought you liked me." Laura laughed as she lowered the cart poles to the ground. "Mr. Joe has the saddle in your barn. I'll take Jewel out there and get her tacked up."

As Joe lifted Mary from her chair, his hat fell in her lap. He put her immediately down in the chair to scoop the hat and slip it over his baldness. Then he carried her to where Laura waited with Jewel.

"You really did this for me, Mr. Joe?"

"When Laura came to me with her plan, I liked the idea." Joe stepped up on a mounting block with Mary in his arms and set her in the saddle.

Mary clutched the saddle horn. "I'm on a horse!" she squealed. The horse tensed and turned her head to look at the eruption of glee coming from the saddle.

"Easy, Jewel. Easy." Laura stroked the alarmed horse's neck. "Really, Mary, you should know better. Jewel is super calm. She's even been in a parade following a marching band, but your screeching is scaring her."

"I'm sorry, Jewel. If you only knew how incredible you are." Mary rubbed the mare's neck softly. "I'm riding! I'm riding the most beautiful horse I've ever seen."

Joe smiled as he buckled straps across her thighs, across her calf right below her knee, and around her ankles. Several long gray curly hairs coiled in his bushy eyebrows. They arched in an upside-down *V* when he asked, "Does that feel secure?"

Mary nodded. "This is so amazing. I'm in a chair that walks."

A grinning Laura held the mare steady. "Someday, we will ride together. Can you picture us cantering across the field?"

"I dream of it. Someday, I will ride Illusion over the clouds and to the stars." Mary tightened her grip on the saddle horn as Laura led Jewel forward a few steps. Joe walked by her side with one hand holding her leg protectively.

"Think of it," Mary marveled, "I have four good legs to walk with. What a fantastic day. Makes me want to sing."

"You know you sing off key, right?"

Mary shrugged. "I sing a joyful noise." Jewel twitched a fly off her shoulder. "I understand now what you mean about my muscles moving to keep me balanced in the saddle. Riding is going to make me strong."

"We're golden—unless your papa finds out."

Mr. Joe reached to the horse's bridle and stopped Jewel short. "What do you mean? Didn't you tell me you had her papa's permission when you brought me the saddle to modify?"

"Well, not exactly. He never said she couldn't."

"You're getting off this horse this minute, Miss Mary. I have to tell your papa. I could lose my job over this."

"I'm okay, Mr. Joe. I can do this. Please don't tell Papa. It's not fair for you to lose your job because of me."

Joe scowled and unstrapped Mary none too gently.

"I'll explain all this to Papa as soon as I can show him how good it is for me. I promise."

Pulling her from the saddle, he placed her into the wheelchair and stomped away.

"That's rotten." Laura planted one hand on her hip and kicked the dirt. "What're we gonna do now?"

"We're not giving up. When you pull the saddle, toss it in your buggy and take it home with you."

The next morning, Mary sensed Laura's excitement as she rushed to the porch where Mary waited. "It was on the radio broadcast last night! I was glued," Laura gushed breathlessly.

"What?"

"Lis Hartel won silver in dressage for Denmark in the Olympics! Silver. She beat out all the top men in the world, except one!" Laura caught her breath. "As if that wasn't amazing enough. The whole world found out at the medal ceremony Mrs. Hartel is disabled from polio." Laura grabbed the handles on the wheelchair and leaned right into Mary's face. "She… can't… use her lower legs to ride—at all! Her doctors told her it was too dangerous to ride a horse. She showed them." Laura swung her fist up and over her shoulder. "She's radioactive and my hero."

"Mine too."

"You haven't heard all of it yet. The man who won gold. Wow. I want to marry him." Laura slapped her hands on her cheeks and swooned. "He dismounted from his horse, rushed to her, and carried her to the podium to accept her medal."

"You're making me cry."

"I know. I flood every time I think about it. I wish we could've been there. Think what it means, Mary. If she can ride and win silver, what would stop you?"

"Papa." Clasping her hands behind her head, Mary closed her elbows over her face. "Papa would stop me."

"You need to tell him about Mrs. Hartel. Then, I bet, he would come up with the idea of your riding all on his own. When does your papa come home?"

"I'm not sure. He calls me every night he's away, so I'll ask tonight. He's usually gone four or five days at a time."

"Then we have plenty of time to try out my saddle idea. Mr. Joe won't even know what we're up to, so he can't get in trouble with your papa." Laura winked. "I have a hunch you might like to visit Illusion today, so let's get. We need to come up with a plan to save her."

Mary moaned. "Every day I cross off the calendar without coming up with an idea, we are closer to..." Her voice choked off. "Mrs. Tate is helping me make and freeze cookie dough so we can bake cookies right before the fair, but I've done the math. It's never going to be enough. Not even close."

"My father reminded me, we have a deadline, and he won't let it go. He said it's not right to let the foal hurt." Laura gritted her teeth. "I hate it when he's right."

Mr. Joe walked from the garden, lifted Mary, and set her in Laura's buggy. Then he hung her wheelchair on hooks in the back. With a couple of quick knots to keep it secured, Mary was all set.

"Thank you, Mr. Joe," said Mary.

He nodded, but left them without a word.

Laura edged closer and nudged Mary with her elbow. "He's still mad at us for riding without permission, isn't he?"

"I'd say. He'll never speak to me again if he finds out Papa told me not to ride in the buggy. But how else could I see Illusion?"

"Is he going to tell on us?"

"He started to tell Papa yesterday. But the phone rang, and Papa left on his trip right after."

"I'm sorry I let it slip. Stuff just jumps outta my mouth sometimes."

"We gotta work on a different plan." Mary pinched her bottom lip with her fingers.

Laura tilted her head and tapped her mouth with a finger. "Our farm manager could lift you up on Jewel. Mr. Todd wouldn't know we don't have permission. Maybe I won't mess it up this time. I talk too much, but I can't seem to help it."

"You are kinda chatty, but that's one of the things I like about you."

"What's the other thing?" asked Laura.

"What makes you my most favorite friend is your socks never match—just like mine."

Laura pinched Mary's skirt and lifted it off her boots to uncover one hot pink and one apple green sock. "Nice." She smiled. "At least mine are in the same color family. For an artist, you're really bad at matching colors."

"Life doesn't match, why should socks?" Mary crossed her arms. "Anyway, we should figure out a way to get me in the saddle on our own."

"What if I bring Jewel alongside the buggy? Could you slide over and get in the saddle?"

"I use my arms to move between chairs all the time. I can do it." Mary snapped her fingers.

"Great. You can ride to the foal paddock to see Illusion." Laura unhooked the harness and saddled Jewel. She cued the horse to sidepass next to the buggy. Stepping Jewel forward and back again, she worked to position the mare close to the seat of the cart. Mary grasped her leg and hoisted her foot over the saddle seat. Pushing down with her hands to lift her body, she slid closer to the horse.

With Laura holding the horse still, Mary eased into the saddle and secured the straps. "We did it!" Mary rubbed Jewel's neck. "Good girl."

"That wasn't so bad." Laura sighed her relief.

"I think we have it figured out. I'd like to use the reins today and guide her myself."

Laura's brow wrinkled. "What if she trots?"

"I'll do a one-rein stop. Don't worry. I got this."

"I can't believe you even know what a one-rein stop is. I'll walk beside you, just in case."

Mary clucked to Jewel, and the mare walked on. "I'm riding. I'm really, really, really riding a horse all by myself!" She squealed. The high-pitched shriek startled the steady old mare, and she jumped forward. Mary grabbed for the saddle horn as her head snapped backward.

"Mary, you've got to stop doing that." Laura reached for the reins to steady the horse.

"Guess I shouldn't screech like a pterodactyl. I'm sorry. I got so excited I forgot."

"Not unless you want to fly like one." Laura giggled. "You push even Jewel's limits. She does have a horse brain after all."

"Tell me how Illusion's doing."

"She stands around all day. She never plays like the other foals. When she takes a step, her head bobs down like she could drop to her knees. Come see for yourself." Laura pointed to the outside paddock.

The foal stood in the shade, holding one front leg bent and slightly off the ground. When she nickered, her nostrils fluttered. "She likes me!" exclaimed Mary.

"Sorry to burst your bubble, but she's talking to Jewel."

"Someday, she'll nicker only for me." Mary eased Jewel to the fence and leaned as far as she dared toward Illusion, but she could barely reach her muzzle. "She feels like the cashmere sweater Papa and I gave Mrs. Tate for Christmas." The filly lipped Mary's fingers, making a smacking noise.

Laura scratched the filly at the base of her tail. "That makes her smile."

"So what can we do to raise the money to fix Illusion?"

"You got me. It hurts me to watch her. My father's right. If we can't fix her soon, we have to put her out of her misery."

"How could I ever say goodbye? I can't think about that." Mary's jaw tightened. She kept Jewel walking along the rail in the arena while she concentrated on trying to convince one of her legs to move back a little and press into the horse's side. Neither leg cooperated. When she looked up again, Laura had squeezed through the paddock fence with Illusion. She rubbed the filly's neck and watched Mary.

"If I didn't know you hadn't been riding," Laura called, "I would have said you've been taking lessons for years. Your contact with the reins is soft and sweet."

"Thanks. I've been reading about horses and how to ride since—my library! That's it, Laura. I could sell my library!" Mary took a deep breath and held it for a minute. New energy sparked in her. "Several of my books are collector items. A couple are vintage and cost a lot of money. Some are signed by the author."

Laura's mouth sprang open. "I love the idea, and I hate it too. That would hurt."

"Not as much as watching Illusion die."

"For sure, nothing would hurt as much as that. We could sell them at the fair booth with the cookies. And I have a bunch of books we could sell too."

Mary squeaked. "We have a plan!"

Laura threw her arms around Illusion's neck, and the filly shook her head so hard she flung Laura off. "Guess she's not into cuddling." Laura laughed.

"I see what you mean about her limping. She is hurting." As the foal hobbled a step, Mary said, "Give her withers a good scratch for me."

Laura scratched the foal with all her fingers until the little horse tilted her head and flapped her upper lip. "It's nice to make her happy, even if it's only for a little while."

Mary smiled, watching them. "She's too adorable. We have to find a way to save her."

"We better finish up with your riding before anyone sees us."

"Right. Then let's get me home, so I can make a list of my books and think on how much to charge for them."

"I have an idea!" Laura squeezed through the fence and planted herself in front of Mary. "Why didn't I think of that before? It's perfect."

"What's perfect?"

"Your sketches." She threw her hands up. "They are so good. I bet lots of people would buy them."

"You think they're good enough to sell?"

"Well, yeah. It's like you dust the drawing with the horse's soul."

Mary stroked Jewel's mane. "I'll try anything. But nobody is going to pay real money for art by me."

CHAPTER SEVEN

*M*ary hoped a great idea for saving Illusion would arrive with the rise of the morning sun. As nothing came, she sighed and wrote one more name on her list of horse books. Then she made a wild guess of what it could sell for. Adding up the column brought a tense frown to her face. "I wish my math was wrong. I've never been good at math, but I'm sure I still don't have enough." She spread the sketches across the desk as she waited for Laura.

Laura lugged a box into the library and dropped it with a thud. "I remembered this box of books in the attic that used to belong to my mother and her sister. Look at this book, it's not a horse book, but that won't matter, will it?"

"It's signed. Wow." Mary exaggerated her mouth as she repeated, "Wow." She held it to her chest with her arms wrapped across it. "I think we could get a lot of money for this."

"Mother said a Laura Ingalls Wilder autobiography is rare. She didn't like the idea of selling it, but she said the final decision is Aunt Claire's since it used to be hers." Laura opened the book to a pencil drawing of a girl on a blanket in the tall prairie grasses. "Aunt Claire gave me permission to sell any of them I needed to. She said she'd send my birthday money early, if it would help."

"I wish I had an Aunt Claire."

"She's mine, all mine. Oh. Look what I got for you." Laura lifted a huge, reddish brown textbook from the box. "Miss Dann. I love her. Ordered it for us from the veterinarian college. You need to read this section on the club foot."

"Thanks. Wow, it's heavy. I want to read it now."

"We should get ready for the sale first." Laura scanned Mary's book list. "You have a signed copy of *The Black*? No way should you sell it."

Mary pointed a finger to the right and followed the motion with her head. "Illusion." Flipping to the left, she said, "Or *The Black*?"

"You're right," Laura agreed. "What am I thinking?"

"Maybe you could take my list of books to show Miss Dann. She might know what they are worth."

"That's a great idea. She's so nice; I know she will help us."

Mary moved a pile of drawings across the polished wooden table to Laura. "Help me pick out some sketches."

"When do we start baking the cookies?" Laura searched through the drawings.

"Tomorrow morning, first thing. Papa should be home tomorrow, so he'll be surprised."

"In a good way, I hope. I'm sure he'll be proud of you for all this."

"I'm not holding my breath. He doesn't get I'm doing what I have to do."

The next day Mary waited on the porch as the evening sky blushed pink. It was almost dark when Papa got home. He closed the door to his car and strode to the porch. "Hello, my Mary. What's that wonderful smell?"

"Papa! I'm so glad you're home. I have tons to tell you."

"You don't have to yell. I can hear you fine." Even his voice smiled at her.

Mary straightened her back and lowered her voice. "Laura and I have come up with a plan to raise money to pay for Illusion's surgery. I reserved a booth at the fair to sell cookies tomorrow. Laura and I have been baking with Mrs. Tate all day."

"Good for you." Papa nodded along as her words rushed out.

"Will you help us tomorrow? We have to take tables and lots of things to set up the booth."

"Tables? How many tables do you need to sell cookies?"

"Three. One for cookies, one for books, and one for my art. Laura is clever or crazy. Maybe both. She thinks my sketches are so good they will raise a lot of money."

"Laura sounds like a girl who knows fine art when she sees it. I guess you have a few books you don't need anymore."

"Well, yes, sort of. Laura brought books from her collection too. She has a signed book called *Little House In The Big Woods*."

"A girls' classic. Should fetch a good price. I'm surprised her parents will let her sell it."

"I guess they understand Illusion is worth it to Laura and me." Mary crossed her arms, uncrossed her arms, and crossed them again. "We're going to hang a sign on the table to tell people we're raising money to save a foal. Most of the sketches for sale are of Illusion and her dam."

"I'm impressed and proud of you, Mary. You are resourceful and determined." He patted her knee. "I'm starving. What do you say we go see what Mrs. Tate has for dinner, besides cookies?" Papa stood and opened the door to the house.

A sweat broke out on Mary's forehead. "Wait, Papa. I have something else."

"My word! What is this?"

"P–Papa," Mary stammered. "These are for the sale tomorrow."

"You cannot sell everything in the house to do a surgery on that foal." He let the door slam.

"No, I wouldn't do that. These boxes are my books. I didn't want to tell you like this."

"There is no good way to tell me something like this—ever." Papa slapped his hat down on top of one of the boxes. "You can't sell your horse book collection. Most of those are your legacy from your mama."

"It's my collection. You said so yourself." Her jaw jutted forward.

"Don't play semantic games with me, young lady."

"I love them, but if selling them can save Illusion, then I have to sell them."

"Over my dead body!" He bent at the waist to look her in the eye.

"What about Illusion's dead body?"

"You are incorrigible. I won't allow it, Mary."

"Are they my books or not?"

Papa's face twisted red and tight. "Yes, yours. To keep, to treasure—not to sell."

"I have to. It's my only choice."

Mary cheered for the sun in the morning because rain would have ruined everything. As she arrived in the kitchen for breakfast, Mrs. Tate finished wrapping sandwiches.

"I've made some lunch for you and Laura," Mrs. Tate said.

"Thank you. At least you understand." Mary folded her hands in her lap and pressed her fingers together. "I had a terrible fight with Papa last night."

"This is harder on him than you realize. He misses your mama, and selling things she loved is painful for him." She slid brownies into the brown paper lunch bags. "I know you don't remember much about your mama. You were so little when she died." Mrs. Tate slid her hand on top of Mary's. "You know the cedar chest by the window in his room?"

Mary nodded.

"It's full of your mama's treasures and precious things he's kept all these years to remember her by." Mrs. Tate leaned toward Mary, her voice almost a whisper. "Are you sure about this? You could have serious regrets."

She shrugged and looked away. "You're right. Mostly what I know about Mama is what you've told me. Papa tries to talk about her sometimes, but he never gets past saying, 'she was an angel.' I love my books, but what else can I do?" With a deep sigh, Mary asked, "Where is he?"

"He went out."

"He wasn't supposed to go to El Paso until next week."

"He didn't say one word to me this morning. I'm worried." Mrs. Tate pulled a plate out of the oven and placed it in front of Mary. "Mr. Joe almost has the truck loaded, so best eat your breakfast."

Mary pushed the eggs around the plate and mashed the cinnamon banana pieces with her fork. "He left me?" she whispered. Her eyes lost focus as the sunlight fractured her pooling tears.

Mary waited at the fair booth by her pile of boxes as Joe unfolded the tables' legs. "There you go, Miss Mary. Good luck."

Laura hurried toward them. She clutched a book in her arms. "I wasn't sure I should even bring this, but it's best if you decide." She extended Mary's treasured copy of *Black Beauty*.

Mary nodded and took the book, gently stroking the cover.

Laura flipped the tablecloth over a table and arranged the cookie trays. "Want me to tape up the sign I made?"

"That would be great. Let's display the art in the middle with the sign, then the cookies and books on either side."

"No second thoughts?" Laura asked.

"Lots of them. If you have any other ideas, I'd jump at anything."

"I wish."

By the time the girls had the items for sale spread out, people crowded the fairgrounds. Music from the carousel horse ride tinkled cheerfully nearby. Mary extended her arm, holding her most loved book and suspended it in the air. With a deep exhale, she finally placed *Black Beauty* on the table with the other books. Nothing could be spared, and nothing was left to do now except hope and pray lots of people would buy art, cookies, and books.

"Mary, I have some extra-bad news."

Mary looked hard at Laura. "What?" she snapped.

"I grabbed carrots for Illusion and sneaked to the barn last night. Father was standing outside Illusion's stall with Mr. Todd. He said he couldn't allow this to go on any longer." Laura stared at her toes. "He told Mr. Todd to make a vet appointment. 'It's time to end it,' he said."

"But he gave us six weeks!"

"Only if she didn't get worse. She's worse."

"What did you do?"

Laura hung her head. "Nothing. I was so shocked. Father wouldn't listen to me anyway. I ran back to the house, and they never knew I was there. I'm a coward, and I let you down. I let Illusion down."

"I was there when you raced to save the driver from the truck that crashed. I've watched you gallop across the fields and leap that massive tree jump. A coward—no way. Anyway, if anybody's let Illusion down, it's me."

Laura bit her upper lip, nodded, and her eyes closed on her pain.

Most people strolled past the booth without stopping. Some looked casually at the offerings. After an hour, they'd sold a couple cookies and one sketch. A girl in an upper grade from Laura's school searched through the books for an eternity before she bought a fiction book about a rescue horse.

"I've always hated that book," Mary confided.

Laura flashed a puzzled look.

"It has a scene where a lady goes out to the barn in the middle of the night to put a blanket on a sleeping horse."

"That's dear."

"The horse is wild, and the lady can't get near it in the daytime. I'm supposed to believe the horse is going to sleep through that. That scene makes me crazy."

"You're right. That couldn't happen."

A few minutes later, the girl returned with a friend who bought a trilogy about girls at a dressage horse show barn and a book of mustang photographs.

"Why aren't people buying my art? I knew it wasn't any good." Mary grabbed one of the sketches, crumpled it into a rock, and pitched it to the ground. "I'm kidding myself. I can't sell enough to save Illusion."

Laura spread her fingers and smacked her hand down on the sketches. "Stop. Just stop."

Mary nodded and bowed her head. Her fingers balled up the fabric of her cotton skirt.

Three boys zigged past them. One boy made a face, snatched a cookie, and disappeared into the crowd.

"I'm telling your mother, Davy," Laura yelled after him.

"I'll pay for it," said a tall, thin woman approaching the table. Her brown hair twirled neatly into a bun at the nape of her neck.

Laura sprang up to hug her. "Miss Dann. I'm so excited you're here."

"Thank you for all your help," Mary said.

"It's what I love. Books and horses. How's the sale going?"

Laura answered with a shrug. "Not great."

Miss Dann picked up a sketch. "This is nicely done, Mary. Save it for me, because I want it." She pointed to an art booth nearby. "I'm going to wander the fair. I'll be back."

Mary and Laura nibbled on their sandwiches at the booth, afraid to miss even a single customer. Two girls carried between them a crispy, fried funnel cake. Laughing, they licked white sugar from their fingers. But Mary's gaze whisked past the donut and followed Miss Dann. "She doesn't walk. She floats. You didn't tell me she was so pretty."

"Prettiest librarian—ever."

After lunch, cookies were the best seller, and soon they were gone. "We've hardly sold any books. Cookies can't pay for surgery." Mary sighed, and her shoulders drooped. "This has to work! Let's count how much money we've made."

Laura counted and recounted. The look on her face was all the answer Mary needed. "What are we going to do?"

"What's left after you've tried everything?"

A woman with a big-brimmed hat examined the drawings. "I see from your sign you hope to save this foal in the sketches. That's a worthy cause, and I'm happy to help." She tucked the art into her bag. "She is precious."

Laura's throat tightened. Her voice cracked. "She means the world to us."

Another woman with long gray hair in a tight braid picked up *Black Beauty*. Mary's eyes blurred as the woman selected her precious book. The woman's wrinkled hands opened the book and flipped the pages. She paused, admiring the artwork. "Lovely book. I had a copy as a girl, but I don't know what became of it."

Laura pointed to Papa, weaving through the crowd, headed toward them.

"I'm tempted," the woman continued. "It's marked quite high. I'll think about it."

"It's signed by Anna Sewell's mother," Mary explained. "She was Anna's caretaker because she had an accident that left her lame."

The lady replaced the book on the table. "That's interesting. Maybe I'll come back a little later."

"It's a collector's..."

Laura pinched Mary's arm to shush her. "Thank you, anyway."

Mary strained to see Papa around the masses of people milling about. "Your papa! Does he look angry?" Laura asked.

"He looks... intense."

Papa removed his cap and stood squarely in front of the tables, scanning the sale items for a long moment.

"Papa, I have to," Mary whispered. She waited as if in a trance. The crowd still moved around her, but they were a mere blur of color and voices. The music tinned to her ear.

As he snapped his cap back onto his head, the commanding sound of his booming voice cut through her daze. "I'd like to buy a book, please. How about the one called *Black Beauty*?"

Mary's face warmed. Her hand covered her mouth, and joyful tears gushed from her eyes.

"I'd also like to have these two books. And this one."

"Oh, Papa, You love me," she blubbered.

"In fact, I think I need a small box. Make it a big box. Actually, I'll take all the books, so I need a truck." Papa leaned over the table toward Mary. "Can you arrange delivery, young lady?"

Mary and Laura both bawled and hugged each other. People passed by staring at them.

Mary rolled her chair to Papa and slid her hand into his. "Where did you go this morning, Papa?" Her voice barely cracked a whisper. "I thought you'd left me?"

"Mary! I would never leave you." He squatted to look directly into her eyes. "You are what keeps my heart beating· I ask myself all the time what would your mama do with you. I finally drove over to the Athens cemetery to talk to her." He took Mary's hands and rubbed them with his thumbs. "Then I knew what I had to do. I'm sorry I let you suffer through worrying about what would happen to Illusion. If your mama were still alive, she would be making as much effort to save the foal as you are." He kissed her fingers and held them to his cheek. "If it was the only way, she would have hawked the books herself."

As her mouth puckered up again, Mary's tears flowed. She threw her arms around him and buried her face in the crook of his neck. She sniffled and wiped her eyes. "I'm so afraid, Papa. I'm so afraid we're too late. She's limping more every day. Laura's father told Mr. Todd they can't wait any longer and to call the vet."

"Then we better get busy," Papa called out to people. "Support a worthy cause, ladies and gentlemen." He waved art in the air. "Buy a sketch of a foal and save the little horse's life."

The girls wiped their eyes as they reached out to collect money handed to them even by people who didn't take a sketch.

Papa's energy gathered a crowd, all with outstretched hands to accept the art. He froze. Miss Dann's skirt swished around her legs as she moved toward him. His hand hung in midair, extending a drawing of Illusion toward her. It was as if the noise and bustle of the fair vanished. She smiled and looked down. He stammered a "hello" which Mary could barely hear.

Laura looked at Mary. Wide-eyed, Mary looked at Laura. Their heads snapped to look at Papa and Miss Dann.

"She likes him," breathed Laura.

Mary bent closer to Laura and whispered, "He likes her more. I can't believe this."

"I think it's sweet."

"You would." Mary scowled.

Miss Dann's lace handkerchief floated to the grass. Papa scooped it up, stepped closer, and placed it gently in her hand.

"He's touching her." Laura pointed.

Miss Dann glanced away, and then up into his eyes. Papa laughed at something she said, leaned a little closer, and whispered to her.

"Is she flirting? I think she's flirting."

"He's flirting too. Your papa's smitten," Laura teased.

71

As Miss Dann walked away, she cast a smile over her shoulder. She clutched a sketch rolled up like a scroll. Papa stood with his back to Mary. His fingers worked around the brim of his hat as he watched her go.

"Drool! I better do something before he runs after her."

"Your papa's smitten," Laura sang and giggled.

CHAPTER EIGHT

That night Mary waited for the house to grow quiet. When the door to Papa's study clicked closed, she peeked into the hall. A dim light filtered under his door. In slow motion, she rolled past it. Putting her ear to the door, she listened for him. Papers rustled, and a pen tapped on the desk. Satisfied he was occupied, she edged forward. As the chair tire bounced on a rough spot, she grimaced and held her breath. After a minute, her heart slowed again, and she inched toward his bedroom. Maneuvering through, she eased the heavy door to lay against the frame. His bedside lamp softened the room's edges. A woodsy scent hung lightly in the air, reminding her she was intruding on Papa.

She stared at the cedar chest against the window overlooking the gardens. It had been a fixture in her life without her realizing its significance. Her finger traced the wood's red grains, polished to perfection. She opened the lid, inch-by-inch; terrified it would squeak and alert Papa.

With both hands, she eased out a dainty, gold-satin hat. Black ostrich feathers overlaid its wide brim and rippled under her fingers. Tucked sweetly inside the hat rested a white handkerchief embellished with miniature, tatted-lace flowers. She placed the hat softly on her head and tilted it for style—transforming her into a lady. A tissue-wrapped package crinkled as she pinched it, folding it away to uncover a veil. Beneath the veil nestled a pair of white satin gloves. Pearls, that had long since yellowed, studded the soft fabric. Mary slipped the gloves on, and they bunched up over her elbows. Rubbing her hands on her gloved forearms, she hugged herself.

From the bottom of the chest, she lifted a Bible. The pages plopped open to reveal a dried, pressed flower. "Ah." It looked white, but she suspected it had once been pink blush. She peered into the garden's darkness toward the pink blush camellia bush. The flower in her hand explained why her papa dug up the plant to take with them every time they moved.

On a dedication page, a feminine scrawl recorded a wedding date. Mary's birth was celebrated, and her christening—"set aside for the Lord" on June 20. Strong print lettering documented the date, March 21, 1944, with no other notation. She didn't have to be a genius to know that was the day her mama died.

A sudden disturbance of the air in the room caused Mary to look up and over her shoulder. Papa stood with his hand on the knob, his face a blank white mask. Her eyes pleaded with him to forgive her for peeking into his heart where she had not been invited.

He came across the room, removed the Bible from her lap, and knelt beside her. Turning to Psalms, he slipped out a slightly tattered photo and placed it in her hand. In the photograph, her papa stood behind a couch and stared directly at the camera. Mother and daughter, however, ignored the photographer. They were otherwise occupied with an intimate moment as they shared smiles. For the first time, Mary understood the enormity of her loss. As her body crumpled, he drew her close and held her tight.

"I know." He stroked her hair. "I know. She loved you deeply and dearly."

Mary bit down on her lip. "Tell me about her."

Papa sighed. "She was beautiful. Inside and out. Every inch a lady. She was always grateful and appreciative. While she was gentle and kind, when it came to watching over you, she had the heart of a warrior." His fingers rubbed Mary's arm. "This is really Mrs. Tate's story to tell, but you can get her to fill in the details later. You would have been… almost three. You and your mama were outside enjoying a spring day. As you played with your doll on a quilt in the grass, your mama stepped into the kitchen to get a cup of peppermint tea. She watched you through the window as the kettle heated. A wild dog crept on its belly toward you. We'd heard it had killed several neighborhood cats and wiped out a flock of chickens." His arms tightened around her. "Though she was only a few steps from you, the dog got there first and snatched you by the dress. It growled and shook you as it dragged you across the grass. You were screeching in terror."

Mary's fingers clutched his shirt as she huddled into him.

"Your mama raced after that dog, grabbed it with her bare hands. One hand on its neck and one hand at the base of its tail. As it yelped, she flung it. Mrs. Tate says over the moon." Papa chuckled. "She was the most amazing woman—your mama." He took the picture from Mary's hand. "She was an angel, so I guess she is exactly where she belongs."

Mary wrapped her arms around his neck and laid her head on his shoulder. "You'll always have me, Papa." She tugged on the folds of his warm jacket. "Why did I live when the virus killed Mama?"

Papa didn't answer and just rubbed her arm. Finally, he said, "Maybe it's time you knew."

She leaned backward and looked up at him.

"The virus ran rampant in East Texas at the time with devastating consequences. I knew a researcher at The Mercy Hospital in Houston who was working on an experimental immune therapy cure. My friend had one minuscule culture. He was certain it could save one of you, but not both. Your mama and I discussed the ramifications at length. You were so very sick, and without something immediately, we knew you would die." He tilted his head to look down at her. "We decided we didn't have anything to lose and took a chance it could save you. She was completely bedridden by then, so I gathered you up and took you to the hospital. My friend secretly administered the immune therapy shot. We could tell no one because it would have meant the end of his career and jail time."

Papa sighed deeply and shook his head. "Mrs. Tate nursed you day and night at considerable risk to her own health. It took about three days before we had hope you would survive. Your mama was sleeping most of the time. I carried you in to see her, and for a moment, she opened her eyes and smiled with joy. She knew you would live, and she passed away in my arms in complete peace later that same day."

Mary curled into Papa's shoulder.

"The tragedy is there was so much love between the three of us that hadn't been shared yet."

Several long minutes later, Papa squeezed her. "Nice hat. Gloves are a little big though."

Mary smiled. "You're the best, Papa."

CHAPTER NINE

*T*he next day, Papa came into the library to tell Mary goodbye.

"Papa. Did you hear the news from Helsinki, Finland about the equestrian team?"

"Why would that be on my radar? No."

"The first woman to ever compete in Olympic Dressage won silver."

"That would please your mama no end. She wished she could compete at that level."

"Was Mama really good? I wish I could have seen her ride. And she could have taught me."

"Yes, in a perfect world." Papa looked out the window in a fixed stare.

"The lady who won silver was disabled from polio. Silver, Papa!"

Papa's attention snapped back to her. "She's a grown woman and can make risky decisions if she wants to, but I have a responsibility to do what's best for you." His finger pointed at her. "I know what you're thinking. Hear me loud and clear. No way will I allow you to ride." He moved directly in front of her. "You understand me?"

Mary dropped her gaze to her hands clasped together in her lap, bit her lip, and nodded.

"If we understand each other then, I'll be home in time to take you to Laura's farm, so we can be there when the vet comes to reassess Illusion. I have a few quick things I need to do in town today."

"And then we can schedule the surgery, and everything will be perfect." Mary crossed her arms on her chest, sat straight in her chair, and stared at Papa.

"I think cautious optimism would be more realistic."

She sat tall and dared to look Papa in the eye. "You'll not discourage me, Papa. We have the money for the surgery now, and we need to get it done right away."

"When I talked to the veterinarian, he was not very encouraging about the surgery's outcome."

"Well," she huffed. "My prayers count more than his opinions."

Papa's lips fluttered as he exhaled. "What am I to do with you?"

"Papa, I've hunted everywhere for Mama's carved horse. Do you know where she is?"

"Let it go, Mary. Put the broken behind you. Be grateful and look to the possibilities." He kissed the top of her head and left.

He knew all along. She watched him go. When her attention returned to the present, she pulled some of her horse books from one of the boxes still stacked along the wall. As she shelved them, she waited for time to pass. She opened the *Complete Equine Veterinarian Handbook* she'd gotten from Miss Dann at the Hunt Library. Running her finger down the table of contents, she found a chapter called, "Deformities Of The Hoof And Leg". Almost two hours of reading later, she folded the book closed. It sounded grim. There could be no more delay. Illusion was getting worse and had to get treatment now.

What was keeping Papa? As she spun the wheels on her chair to hurry to the porch, he eased out of the car.

"I was afraid you'd be late, and we would miss the vet."

"Mary, do I let you down so much you have reason to doubt me?"

She shook her head, rubbed her thumb in the palm of her hand, and muttered, "No, Papa. I'm sorry." Mary put her hands together over her heart. "Even if I can never ride her, something in here will die if we can't save Illusion."

"If the worst comes to pass with Illusion, it's still a bump in life's road. No more. You hurt, you pray, you heal, and you move on."

"Are you healed?"

"Healing is a process. I had an important job." He dropped on a knee in front of her and swallowed her hands in his. "I had to take care of you, and that gave me purpose and got me through."

Mary leaned on his shoulder and hugged him. "I love you, Papa."

Mary and Papa rode to Laura's farm without talking. She never diverted her eyes from the road. The veterinarian's truck was parked in front of the barn, and Laura waited next to it. Laura hurried to them. "I'm so glad you're here."

"What's going on? How's she doing?" Mary asked as Papa unloaded her chair.

Laura bit her lip, shook her head, and looked back at the barn as Laura's mother and the veterinarian disappeared into the barn.

"Hurry, Papa." Mary tilted forward and strained to help propel her chair till they were flying down the barn alleyway.

The veterinarian, Laura's father and mother, and Mr. Todd stood looking into the stall at Illusion. As Mary, Laura, and Papa joined them, Laura's father motioned for Mr. Todd to bring the filly out into the alleyway. The foal pulled against the halter so hard she almost sat on her haunches. Shaking her head, she planted three feet, held one dainty hoof high, and refused to budge. Laura's father popped the foal's rump with a quirt, and she jumped onto the concrete. Her head lunged all the way down to her hoof and snapped back up. One hopping step and then two.

The foal was in such terrible pain Mary could feel it in her own bones. "Stop!" she blurted. "Stop! You're hurting her."

The veterinarian turned to Mary. His thick tanned skin hardened his face, but his eyes smiled and gentled his mouth lines. "I have to see how she's walking, and I can't give her anything to mask the pain until I'm finished with my exam. I'm sure it hurts you to watch this. Perhaps it would be best if you waited outside."

"No, sir, I'm sorry. I understand. I so hate that she's hurting."

"I hate it too, and I won't let her hurt any longer than absolutely necessary." He placed a hand on her shoulder. "We may have to make a hard, grown-up decision today."

A silent scream echoed in Mary's head. She covered her ears with the heels of her hands and pressed to block out the toxic news.

The veterinarian's attention returned to Illusion as he ran both hands down her front leg. "The curvature of her leg doesn't seem any worse than the first time I saw her. But her leg is markedly more swollen, and I detect a little heat in her hoof." He lifted her tiny hoof and tapped the bottom of it with a small mallet. "Hum," he said as he walked away. "I'm going after a hoof tester from my truck."

Mary and Laura reached for each other's hand and held tightly.

"She's so much worse. I hate what I'm thinking," Laura said.

"I know what you're thinking. You think we have to do the best thing for her no matter how much it hurts us." Mary squeezed Laura's hand. "And you might be right. She's in agony." Both girls kept their eyes riveted on the foal. Mary let go of Laura and reached both hands toward Illusion. The horse's nose extended, reaching toward her. "Will you forgive me, Illusion? I don't know what else to do."

"What a shame. A horse with such kind eyes and yet so much spirit and spunk. She would have been a great friend for you," Laura said.

"I don't know if I can say goodbye." Mary ran her fingers through Illusion's forelock. Pulling the ribbon from her own ponytail, she tied a little pink bow between the filly's ears.

The veterinarian returned, lifted the hoof again, and squeezed it with a metal, pincer-like tool. Illusion squealed, jerked her hoof away, scrambled to get free, and fell to the concrete. The girls gasped in unison.

"I'm going to be sick." Mary spun her chair around and raced away as fast as she could toward the fresh air. Laura hesitated and then chased after her. Once outside, the girls burst into tears. Mary's chest heaved, and her stomach knotted.

Laura covered her face with both hands and dropped to her knees in the grass. "This can't be happening."

When the men came outside, both girls turned away. Mary's stomach ached from sobbing.

"Mary," Papa said. "Listen to me. We have an important decision to make."

"I know. I hate it, but yes. We can't let her hurt anymore." Mary's lips wrinkled in a pout. "Do what you have to do."

"Mary, you don't understand. The veterinarian thinks there is a possibility the reason for Illusion's increase in pain is she might have an abscess in her hoof."

Mary sniffled and stopped crying. "That's not so bad."

Laura looked up and came nearer.

Papa hovered over her. "The vet says it's possible she stepped on something sharp and developed a pocket of infection in her hoof. He said, in her case, the best way to confirm an abscess is to do tests at the Texas Equine Hospital. Even if she does have an abscess causing the extreme pain, she still has the issue of the clubfoot. It's hard to separate one problem from another."

"Are you saying even if we do the tests and she has an abscess, it still might not make any difference to her?" Mary asked.

"Yes, I'm afraid so. We might be prolonging her suffering."

Mary grasped Laura's hand. "We should pray."

Laura nodded. They bowed their heads, and Papa watched with his cap in his hand.

As the veterinarian walked to his truck with Laura's father, he asked the girls, "Do you have any questions for me?"

Mary's and Laura's eyes met and held. Laura shook her head.

"I have to see Illusion." Mary lifted her chin as she turned to ask her papa. "Can I have a few minutes alone with her?"

He nodded. Fearing the veterinarian would try to change her mind, Mary rushed off to Illusion's stall.

Mr. Todd stepped out of the stall, leaving the door open for Mary. He scooped the calico barn cat out of her way. The filly stood on three legs with the hoof of her right front balanced on the toe. As the pain medication took effect, the foal's head and neck drifted lower.

With the calico tucked in one arm, Mr. Todd extended a miniature brush to Mary. Her eyes held his as she took it from his hand. It occurred to her, she was wrong about Mr. Todd. She eased her chair into the stall and stroked the filly's neck with the soft brush.

Her fingers reached for and entwined in Illusion's thin, baby mane. Her forehead rested against the filly's face. "We would have been amazing together, but how cruel it would be to let you hurt because I need you so much." With both their eyes closed, Mary hummed to the foal as tears flowed down her cheeks and wet Illusion's face. "No matter what happens, I will always, always love you. Don't be afraid. Mrs. Tate said God himself would take care of you." Mary sniffled. "Please forgive me."

The next morning Papa pushed the door open to the library. Mary's hands were limp in her lap as she sat motionless by the window. Not a breath of air stirred—as if the whole world waited for the results of Illusion's tests.

"Let me guess what occupies your mind this morning."

"You know," Mary whispered.

"We should hear from the equine hospital today."

Mary nodded, but continued to stare vacantly out the window.

"Want me to return the vet book to Charlotte?"

"Charlotte?"

"Miss Dann."

"No. No, thank you. Laura will take it to school and return it." Mary straightened her back. "You could never love anyone else like you loved Mama, right?"

"Of course not. That's an odd question from you."

"It's been a little odd around here."

"Do you want me to take you out to your spot so you can sketch today?" Papa encouraged her.

Mary held back a little secret. "No," she said. "Laura is coming to cheer me up, and she's going to help me put the books back on the shelves."

"Is there something else?" Frowning, Papa took a step closer. "What are you not telling me? Withholding something is the same as lying."

"Nothing," she lied, turning to look at him. "Nothing at all." It was wrong, completely wrong, this should happen today of all days. How could she have something good to share when she expected the worst news about Illusion? She couldn't tell Papa until she was sure anyway.

"You keep doing the strength exercises, and I will see when we can return to Destin." He kissed her cheek. "I'm off." The front door shut behind him.

Turning to the window, she sighed. "Hurry, Laura? I can hardly wait to show you." Spinning her chair, she wheeled herself to the kitchen to find Mrs. Tate.

"French toast. My favorite. You love me."

"Yes, actually, I do. As vexing as you can be, I love you dearly." Mrs. Tate smiled and wiggled her nose like a bunny.

As a bite of French toast melted in her mouth, Mary cut the rest into small pieces to make it last.

"Mr. Gregory called. He has to travel to Canaan this morning. He said to tell you, he'll still come for your tutoring today."

"I'll go to Laura's then. She should be here soon anyway. I'll be back in time for lessons." Mary watched Mrs. Tate's face to see if she knew yet riding in the buggy was forbidden.

"Why isn't Laura in school?"

"She's been on spring break this week. She gets off early every afternoon anyway because she has a job on her family farm."

Mary breathed a huge sigh of relief it wasn't the buggy ride on Mrs. Tate's mind.

"Mrs. Tate, with all this happening with Illusion, I've been thinking." She bit her lip and looked into Mrs. Tate's eyes. "I told Illusion what you said about God taking care of her and all, but death is like, you know, it's all over. I'm scared for Illusion."

Mrs. Tate balanced a wooden spoon on the glass mixing bowl and gazed out the kitchen window. "I think dying is like being born in the first place. Before you were born, you were in a comfortable, safe place." She folded the chocolate batter a couple times with the spoon. "You didn't know anything about what it would be like when you were born into the world. Look how it turned out."

"You're right, this world is amazing. Lying in the water at the beach, I had a lot of time to just look at stuff. The details on the birds. The shells on the beach."

"God is an artist. He created this place for us as a picture of an even more glorious heaven."

"I don't want Illusion to leave me."

"Our life here is but a wisp." She wagged the spoon at her. "Make sure you enjoy the gift."

Mary reached into the bowl with a teaspoon and snagged some batter. Turning the spoon upside down, she smoothed it across her tongue.

Mrs. Tate rapped the bowl with the spoon and waved it at Mary. "Brownies are for later, not breakfast."

"You're the one who said 'enjoy the gift'." Mary giggled. "I hear hoof beats. Must be Laura. Gotta go." Mary stopped in the doorway. "Thanks, Mrs. Tate. I never thought of dying like being born into a better place."

CHAPTER TEN

*M*ary drummed her fingers on the arm of the chair while she waited for Laura to tie up Jewel. She couldn't quite hide the little smug smile tugging at the corners of her mouth.

Laura took one look at Mary and asked, "What's up? Something's up. I know you, Mary, and something's up."

"Come with me." Mary led the way into the library. "Shut the door," she whispered.

Laura eased the door shut and plopped into the pink stuffed chair. "Remind me to tell you what happened with my mother. Now, what has you so jazzed?"

"I haven't even told Papa or Mrs. Tate yet." Mary's smile spread across her whole face. "I stood up this morning."

"Really, Mary? That's fantastic!"

"I can hardly believe it."

"The riding—do you think?"

"Yes. My muscles have gotten stronger. Papa never misses a day to remind me to do Dr. Krane's exercises, and the ones you taught me to do in the saddle are helping. But I'm afraid to tell Papa. He's already talking about going back to Florida, and I can't think about that now. I have to be here with Illusion through it all." Mary sighed. "Watch." With the wheels locked, she balanced on the edge of her chair. Putting weight on her legs, she leaned forward. Pressing her feet into the floor, she lifted herself out of the chair. "No hands." She dropped down and repeated the motion. "Soon I will ride like a free spirit escaped from a trap."

Laura threw both hands up with her fingers spread open as wide as her mouth. "Oh my, that's boss. Look at you! It's like you're posting in a saddle!" Laura squeaked.

"Incredible, huh? Can you believe it? I can only do it a couple times, but I'm getting stronger every day. If only Illusion... we would be amazing together."

"We will find you the right horse someday. For now, I don't think we should sit here and watch the clock tick. That won't help Illusion. Let's go ride."

When Laura had Jewel tacked up, she brought the horse out of the barn and lined her up next to Mary, still sitting in the buggy. "I decided I would ride with you today on Treasure. He needs something to do, and he earned a break from being Illusion's babysitter."

"Our first ride together. Let's post."

"Might be best to start with a slow trot. But the posting trot should be easier on a horse than in a wheelchair. The horse's motion gives you a little bounce. I think Jewel could follow behind Treasure, and he would keep her steady."

"I'm so excited."

Laura grinned. "Me too. Are you going to slide over or not?"

Mary lifted her foot and scooted across the bench seat until she settled into the saddle. She tucked the fabric of her skirt around her legs so they wouldn't stick to the leather.

"We've got to get you riding pants." Laura pushed Mary's feet solidly into the stirrups.

Mary smiled at the thought of her own jodhpurs. "I could wear them under my skirt so Papa wouldn't notice. I feel a little guilty riding without telling him, but soon I'll be able to show him. The more I ride, the stronger I get. When I can walk, nothing will stop me from saving Illusion." She did a happy chicken dance with her elbows while she belted out a tune. "I feel good, da-da, da-da, da-da, da!" Mary smiled as big as the Texas sun. "This is gonna work. I know it."

"Oh stop! Even singing lessons won't help you. You're silly today. At least you're not totally gloomed about Illusion."

"I'm faking it some. Illusion is all I can think about, but I'm trying not to believe the worst." Mary grimaced. "Or watch the nightmare motion picture, playing in my brain, of Illusion being forced to walk yesterday."

"Wasn't that awful?"

"It all looks hopeless, and it gets worse every day." Mary took in a deep breath and blew it out in a puff. "Hurry, get Treasure. We don't have much time."

Laura disappeared into the barn to tack up Treasure and soon trotted into the arena. The girls rode side by side along the rail. The horses' heads hung low and relaxed. Jewel's head popped up, and her ears pointed off to a bushy area when a bird flitted away. Mary automatically lifted one rein to remind the horse she was working. Except for the hooves scuffing along in the sand, the girls rode in silence.

Finally, Laura shortened her reins. "Let's walk patterns. You and Jewel can follow me."

The girls rode in figure eights, three-loop serpentines, and different-sized circles.

"You're doing fine," Laura said. "It will go even better when you can use your legs on her."

"Let's trot."

"If you're sure," Laura said. "Here goes."

Jewel followed Treasure along the arena fence. "Grab some mane, Mary. Don't worry about your diagonals." Both horses eased into a trot.

"Wait," Mary called, and Laura halted Treasure.

"What?"

"I need to unbuckle the straps so I can post."

"A colossal bad idea."

"I can do it. I feel balanced in the saddle. It's all smooth."

"It's a bad idea," Laura repeated and waited for Mary to come to her senses. But Mary unbuckled them anyway. Finally shaking her head, Laura squeezed Treasure into a slow trot and asked him to whoa about every ten steps to look back and check on Mary. "Let the energy of the horse bounce you up and forward. I'll trot farther this time, so you can pick up a better rhythm. Call out if you need me to stop."

"Don't look back at us. I'm a bouncing bullfrog in a saddle."

Laura laughed. "Maybe, but you're still in the saddle. That's what counts."

As they started to trot again, Mary's feet slipped out of the stirrups. With one hand gripping the mane, she dropped the reins and grabbed for the saddle horn. It wasn't enough. The next trot stride pitched her forward. When her body slapped back into the saddle, she lost her balance. Slipping to the side, still clinging to Jewel's mane, she called, "Stop! I'm falling."

Laura pulled a little too hard on Treasure's reins. Jewel swerved to avoid running up on him, flinging Mary completely out of the saddle. Mary dangled around Jewel's neck for an instant before thudding to the ground. Dirt and skirts flew everywhere. Jewel shuffled backward. Mary lay perfectly still.

"Ach… I know what that feels like. Are you all right?" Laura dismounted and ran the few steps to Mary. Pulling Treasure behind her, she knelt beside Mary. "Are you all right? Do you hurt anywhere?"

Jewel skittered away, dragging her reins, snapping them off as she stepped all over them. Head held high, the horse pranced about swinging her mane from side to side. After a loud snort, she wandered to graze the grass along the arena fence line.

Mary groaned. "I'm afraid to move. If I'm not dead, Papa is going to kill me."

"You're not dead. Your papa won't know."

Mary took Laura's offered hand and sat up in the dirt. She stretched her neck, rolled her shoulders, and wiped the dirt off her face. "I think everything checks out okay. Getting dumped gets me in the riders' club right?"

"You weren't dumped. You fell off in slow motion, which is not the same."

"But I'm in right?" Mary asked.

"You're in."

"I should've kept on the saddle straps, but I thought it'd be okay."

"Ya think? They are on there for a reason."

Mary looked around and then at Laura. "Now what?"

"There is no way I can get you up on Jewel from the ground. We need your wheelchair."

"You can't push me in the chair in this sand." Mary thought a minute. "It's too far to crawl."

"What if I get a wheelbarrow? We can move you to the buggy in it. How we are going to boost you up into the seat, I don't know yet. But I'm clever." Laura snickered. "I'll figure it out."

"Do we have any other options?"

"Like what? I could go find the groom to help us. But he'll tell my father."

"Get the wheelbarrow," Mary moaned.

"Jewel seems happy eating grass, so I'll leave her for now." Laura led Treasure off to the barn. Pushing the tarp-covered chariot out to where Mary sat, Laura said, "Your carriage, my lady."

"Do we have a plan for this?"

"We do." Laura whipped the tarp off the wheelbarrow. "If you sit on the tarp, I can drag you to the fence. Since you can stand up for a few seconds, you can use the fence to hold yourself up. I'll squeeze the wheelbarrow underneath you."

"I do not believe this."

Laura laughed. "Give it a whirl. It sounds crazy, but it might work."

"I can't think of a better idea." Mary squirmed and scooted to get in position. "You are very clever, Laura, to think of this. I wish I was as clever as you."

With a corner of the tarp over her shoulder, Laura dragged it to the fence like a workhorse in harness.

With Laura on one side and the fence on the other, Mary struggled to pull herself upright. "I'm standing! Get the wheelbarrow. Hurry."

"Your feet are on the tarp." Laura bent over and tugged the tarp free. In one motion, she snatched the tarp off the ground and flung it across the wheelbarrow. Laura hurried to angle the wheelbarrow down so Mary could sit in it. Not able to hold herself that long, Mary thudded into the wheelbarrow. It tipped to the side dumping her into the dirt and pulling Laura off balance as it went. As Laura tumbled, Jewel exploded in a panic. Fleeing the scene, her hooves plastered dirt over both girls.

"Yes, I feel really clever." Laura spit grit out of her mouth.

Mary hooted. "You look like a leopard Appaloosa."

"Great. Thanks to my carriage horse that spooks at nothing—ever. You are a bad influence on her."

"Okay, clever one, what now?" Mary spread her arms wide. "It better be good. The longer we're out here like this, the closer we are to getting caught. I know my papa. He'll hire a warden-nanny to watch my every move." Mary moaned and flipped sand in the air with both hands.

"This is not my fault!" Laura put her hands on her hips. "Let's skip the tarp."

"That's not a muck cart is it?"

"No! You're already filthy anyway. What if you lean toward the fence as you sit? With the wheelbarrow next to the board, maybe it won't tip over." The two friends tried again. This time, as Mary kerplunked into the wheelbarrow, Laura tipped it back quickly. Mary fell backward and smacked her head.

"That had to hurt," Laura said. "Sorry."

"It's okay." Mary tugged herself up, slid into the wheelbarrow bucket, and rubbed the back of her head. "They had team wheelbarrow races at the fair. We should've entered. We could've been rodeo clowns."

Laura leaned in as the wheels hit a patch of deep sand and huffed as she thumped the wheelbarrow down. "I can't do this. The sand is too deep. I'm whipped."

"I don't know what to do. The buggy might as well be miles away."

"We still have to get you up into it somehow." Laura sat cross-legged in the sand. Her eyes closed.

"You're right." Mary moaned. "I've ruined everything."

Laura's eyes popped open. "You give up too fast. You know I'm clever."

"What? Tell me your idea."

Laura jumped up and swished the sand off her jodhpurs. "I remembered something. My mother hired a trainer from New Zealand to start the two-year-olds once. Jewel was in that herd. He laid them all down to teach them something—I forget what. But I watched, and I might remember the cues he used, though I've never done it. It's been a long time, and Jewel might not remember either."

"So what?"

"If I can lay her down, you could get on, silly." Laura turned on her heel and dashed for the barn, returning with an overflow of carrots and a long training whip. She tossed the carrots to Mary. "Here. Start breaking them up into small pieces."

Laura dragged the tarp to Mary. "We will toss a few onto the tarp so Jewel doesn't eat sand with the carrots. If she has lots to eat while she is laying down, maybe she won't get up too fast."

"You have crossed over from clever to crazy! I'm not getting on. I need to get home. Ask your groom to carry me to the buggy." Mary wiped as much dirt from her arms and face as she could with a petticoat. She shook out her skirt and spread it neatly around her. But instead of getting the groom, Laura caught Jewel.

"My teacher is coming. I have to get home," Mary protested.

"You should have thought of that before you unbuckled your straps. Now, you have to get back in the saddle. You always do that after a fall so you don't lose your nerve."

"I haven't lost my nerve! I just don't have time. Mr. Gregory will be there soon."

"Prove it!" Laura insisted. "Prove you're not chicken."

"I have a knot in my stomach like something bad is about to happen." Mary clenched her fist and pressed it into her stomach.

"See, you are scared. You don't have to ride long. We need to get you past it."

"We don't have time to experiment. You don't know if you can even get her to lay down. I'm going to be found out for sure."

"Oh, we have time. When I went after the whip, I noticed the farm truck is gone. The groom must have gone to the feed store."

"Ugh," groaned Mary as she started breaking up carrots.

Laura positioned Jewel as close to Mary as she dared. She tapped the mare's foot with the whip. The horse lifted the hoof and plopped it right back down. "She knows I want something, but not sure what." At the tap and with a little downward pressure on the rein, the mare dropped to one knee, and Laura slipped a carrot into the surprised horse's mouth. Laura asked the horse to rise again by tapping her hip and repeated the action a couple times. Soon Jewel dropped to her knees with her rump in the air when Laura pointed the whip at her hoof. "I don't remember how to get her to lie down all the way."

"Keep feeding her a few carrot pieces. If she starts to get up, tap her leg so she'll know that's not the right answer. Maybe she'll get tired of holding her rump in the air and eventually lay down. We can give her lots of carrots, and I can crawl on her back while she's eating."

"How did you learn all that from a book? I need to read more." Laura shook her head.

Soon Crown Jewel flopped on her side, and Laura spread oodles of carrot pieces on the tarp. Mary grabbed the saddle horn and pulled. Laura put an arm around Mary and helped tug her into the saddle. Jewel scarfed up all the carrots and stayed on her belly in the sand. Laura tapped the mare on the hip with the training whip, but Jewel waited for the carrot vending machine to dispense more treats. "Oh great. She's found the carrot farm, and she's not leaving." Finally, Laura handed the whip to Mary to use, and Laura tugged on a rein. Working in concert, the girls were able to convince the horse there would be no more carrots and she should get up.

"What do ya say we put the straps on this time?" Laura rolled her eyes.

"Okay, okay. Let's get this over with quick." Mary rode Jewel, and Laura walked alongside. After they walked a lap, Laura encouraged her. "You have good contact with her mouth, so tighten up the reins and try to squeeze with your legs." Jewel eased into a trot—smooth and slow and collected.

"Wow, this is amazing. We should have done this slow trot first."

"Yes, but you wanted to post."

"I love this. What a floating gait she has."

"She wins ribbons with it. Trot to the gate, and we're done."

"What already? One more loop around? This is wonderful fun. Can I ride home like this?"

"No way. And not my fault if your papa finds out you missed your lessons and grounds you for life."

"I'm just joking. I do that when I'm scared. Mrs. Tate is going to be so disappointed in me. Papa is going to be furious. I just know I've messed everything up and I'm in hot, hot water."

CHAPTER ELEVEN

With Jewel back in her traces, Laura guided her toward Mary's farm.

"I forgot!" Mary twisted toward her. "You never told me what happened with your mother."

"I was so excited about your news, I forgot too. And it's like if I don't say it out loud, maybe the bubble won't pop."

"What happened?"

"My mother actually waited for me in the breakfast room this morning. At first, I thought I was in big trouble. But she smiled, got a plate, and sat down with me. That never happens. She is always—*always*—off doing her own stuff."

"What did she say?"

"That she's been watching me fight for Illusion, and she couldn't be more proud of me." Jewel's hooves click-clacked on the road. "She said she realized she's been missing out by making other things more important than me." Laura paused for several trot strides. "She asked me to forgive her for not being the mother she should have been and to let her make it up to me."

"Wow. That's deep."

"She wants to take me shopping and to lunch at a fancy place. Somewhere the two of us can talk, she said."

"Is this really your mother? Amazing."

Laura's smile reflected her new joy, and her eyes glistened. Mary enjoyed both the breeze in their faces and the rhythm of the hoof beats. As Laura's barn disappeared from sight, wood snapped under them. They looked at each other with grimaces and wide eyes.

"Now what?"

The splintering sound mushroomed into a loud crack. The buggy wheel on Laura's side skidded a few feet before the buggy lurched lower. The girls grabbed for the railing as the cart tipped, and Jewel's head shot up as she jolted to a stop.

Gripping the bar, Laura bent over the side to examine the wheel. "Oh no."

"What happened?"

"The wheel is completely wrecked."

"I'm in so much trouble." Mary groaned. "Mr. Gregory will tell Papa I wasn't home, and Papa will know I've been riding in the cart." Mary covered her face with her hands and sputtered like an errant balloon. "What if Papa decides to punish me by not helping Illusion?"

"He would never do that." Laura's mouth wore an exaggerated frown. "Would he?"

Mary squished up her face as if she'd eaten sour candy and nodded.

"What can we do? All that's left of the wheel spokes is splinters, and the rim collapsed."

Mary leaned across Laura and looked over the edge. "Doom." She popped back up. She twisted side to side positive a brilliant idea was on its way. "We need a plan. We can't walk home," she said, stating the obvious.

"I can't push you in your wheelchair all the way home either. We need to teach Jewel to pull your chair like a buggy."

Mary shook her head no. "I think that would work out worse than your last clever plan. We should pray someone will come along and help us." Mary brought her palms together and bowed her head.

The girls sat in the tilted buggy with the busted wheel, peered down the long empty road, and waited.

"Your prayer is not working."

Mary threw her hands up.

"Your prayer about my dream worked though."

"It did? I'm cranked about that."

"I've been praying every night like you told me. And I've not had even one bad dream."

Mary smiled and hugged her friend. "No more bad dreams! That makes me happy." Mary heaved a sigh. "We can't sit here and bake in the sun all day. We better come up with something."

"I'll unhook Jewel and ride her to my farm to see if the groom is back." Laura jumped down and started unbuckling the harness traces.

"Wouldn't he have passed us on the road?"

"Ahh. Yes. That's a no-go."

"I need to go home. Wish we had put the saddle in the buggy. What if we ride double to my farm? I can do it."

"Bareback?" Laura's eyes grew into huge round orbs. "No way. And you think my wheelbarrow plan was bad?"

"I am sure I can do it. My balance is good. Jewel can just walk."

"Says the one covered in dirt from falling off. That's like the worst idea—ever."

"It's my idea and my decision. Should I ride in front or behind you?" Mary asked.

"I need to have the reins." Laura's brow wrinkled. "Can you climb on behind me without pulling me off?"

"Umm…" Mary eyed the horse and nodded. "Leave the harness on, so I'll have something to pull on."

Laura flipped the long lines up over the horse's back and stripped away the breast collar, traces, and crupper. "I'll have to sit right behind the rein terrets—that's not much room for two. A lot of horses would buck us off with you sitting on her loins, but she earned the name Crown Jewel." Jewel tossed her head and started to pull toward home. "No, you don't. I know what you're thinking. Every time I brag on you, you start something." Laura swung up on her back.

"Crown Jewel already dropped me once today, so bucking wouldn't surprise me."

"That wasn't her fault! You should have put your straps on." Laura repositioned the horse close to the buggy.

"Let's stop talking about it and get going." Mary lifted her foot over Jewel's back and slid onto the horse behind Laura. She grinned. "I've always, always wanted to ride with no saddle."

"I'm not taking the bridle off, no matter what you think."

Wrapping her arms around Laura, Mary held tight to the back band of the harness. "It won't take us long to get me home like this. And no one will know."

"We're going to have to leave your wheelchair here on the buggy. Have you figured out how to explain why you don't have it?"

"I didn't think of that. I'll have to ask Mr. Joe to carry me to the house and come get my chair. He's going to come undone. I'm doomed."

"You better come up with a good story about why you're so dirty too."

"I'll think of something. It'll come to me."

As the girls came around the last bend in the road, a black car turned into the farm. "That's Papa! Why is he home so early?"

The girls rode the rest of the way in silence. As they approached the front porch, Mr. Gregory rose from the rocker.

Mary kept her voice low. "It's been nice to know you, Laura. I think I'll never see you again. Kiss Illusion goodbye for me."

"Goodbye, Mary. I'll miss you."

Papa blasted out the front door. He strode to the horse and hauled Mary from its back. "In the name of God, what are you thinking?" His clean white shirt now looked like a young artist finger painted it with grime. As he carried her to the porch, she peered over his shoulder at Laura. Laura gave a tiny wave, quietly cued Jewel to turn around, and headed home.

Papa plopped Mary in a rocker. Bending at the waist, he leaned toward her with his hands on his knees and started to speak, but nothing came out. He wagged his finger in her face, spun away, and kicked a flower basket off the porch. It careened through the air, and zinnia stems scattered across the porch and the grass. Mr. Gregory stood like an awkward boy, mangling his hat in his hands, until he abruptly bounded down the steps and left. Papa slammed his hat on his knee repeatedly as he paced the length of the porch.

Mrs. Tate peeked out from behind the curtains. Mr. Joe inched away to a garden section behind the house.

Papa muttered, sputtered, and grunted.

"I'm sorry. Let me explain," Mary said.

He spun and pointed his finger at her again. "Be. Quiet. I'm not ready to hear anything from you."

His shoes crushed zinnia petals into powder. "I expressly forbid you to ride in the buggy. What possessed you to imagine it was all right for you to ride on a horse?" He stomped and ranted. "I'm astonished you would disobey me like this and risk your life to-boot." He thundered the length of the porch. "To think, I was going to help you with that foal. I can see now what a terrible idea that was."

"Papa."

"You were one of the girls in the buggy the neighbor told me about the day the big truck crashed. I should have realized it was you and Laura. I trusted you. I never imagined… I won't make that mistake again. You will go nowhere without a chaperone from here on out." His voice softened. "You are all I have left in this world." Then boomed again. "I'm horrified to find out what a disobedient child you have become."

"Papa! I have something important to tell you."

"I've tried to be both mother and father to you." His face flushed and his voice roared. "I've spoiled you. Rules are to be obeyed." Poking his finger in her face again, he steamed. "Some things need to change around here. It's time you went to a girls' boarding school." He pivoted away from her and stomped a stinkbug, which had the misfortune to be in the wrong place at the wrong time.

Mary pushed down on the arms of the chair. As she rose, she reached for the railing. "Papa!"

"Your mama would be mortified by your behavior. I've failed her." As he continued to rage, he whirled to face Mary.

His jaw dropped open wide, and he stammered, "Ma–Ma–Mary. You're standing."

She sank into the chair. "That's what I wanted to tell you. Since the trip to Florida, I've been getting stronger. While we were gone, Laura got a book from Miss Dann about equine rehabilitation therapy. She had an old saddle fitted for me with straps and everything."

"You've been riding behind my back all this time! How could you do such a thing? I never would have believed you could be capable of such deceit."

"I'm sorry. You know you would never have allowed it. I tried to tell you yesterday morning in the library. But look at me. The aquatic therapy got me going, and now I'm getting stronger every day. The book Laura got had strength building and balance exercises on horseback." Mary hung her head and tapped her toes together. "I didn't want to get your hopes up. You've done so much to help me get well. And I'm sure now. I'm getting better, and it started at the ocean."

When she looked up, Papa's face softened. He sank into the chair opposite her, put his elbows on his knees and his face in his hands.

A tear flowed down his cheek, and she reached for his arm. He scooped her into a bear hug. "Thank you, God! Thank you." Tilting his head, he searched her eyes. "I should have figured you would try riding after you told me about the disabled woman who medaled in the Olympics. I should have seen it coming." He smiled as he peppered her with questions. "How long can you stand? Can you walk? How could you keep this from me?"

"You know I had to keep it a secret. You would've never allowed me to ride. You wouldn't even let me ride in the buggy. I can't walk yet, but I can stand for about a half a minute." She hugged him around the neck. "Papa, I have something important to ask you."

"Is it about boarding school? I was furious with you, but I can't send you away."

"I know. You'd miss me too much. It's more important than that." Mary cupped her hands over his ear and whispered, "It's the most important thing ever."

"Did I just witness the miracle I've been praying for? You stood up for the first time in eight years. You can ask me anything."

"The therapy in Florida helped me so much." She took in a deep breath for bravery. "I've been reading about aquatic therapy for horses. I know it will help Illusion." Mary paused to see how he reacted before she rushed on. "I want Illusion to have the surgery for her club foot, and then take her to Florida and swim her in the ocean. It's the best chance she has. And I'm sorry for riding in the buggy after you told me not to."

He eased her into the chair. Drawing in a deep breath, he said in a low, quiet voice, "You were wrong to do that. It's important I can trust you." He took hold of both her hands. "I talked to the veterinarian today, which is why I came home early."

She bit her lip at hearing the serious in his tone. "Is it more bad news?" Her face twisted with anguish.

He reached for tissues and handed them to her. "He agrees with you about doing the club foot surgery, and he said Illusion does have a massive abscess or infection in her hoof. Because of the severity, the vet recommended a procedure where he drills into her hoof to allow the abscess to drain."

Mary sniffled but waited for him to finish.

"He's scheduled both surgeries for first thing in the morning."

Mary's fingers interlaced, crushing her tissue, and a thumbnail mashed into the other hand. Her mouth felt like dry cotton when she tried to speak. "Will it hurt her? Will she be... all right?"

"He said of all the hoof ailments horses get, an abscess is the most treatable. He expects a full recovery if we do the proper rehabilitation after the drainage surgery."

Sitting up straighter, Mary asked, "Well, of course, we will. Won't we, Papa?"

"The protocol for the abscess is antibiotics and saltwater soaks."

Mary's hands flew to cover her gaping mouth. "Saltwater?"

"I know what you're thinking, but she doesn't need to go to Florida for an abscess. She can soak in a bucket of Epson Salts in her rubber-mat-lined stall."

Tears welled up again in Mary's eyes. "I'm sure if she could swim in the ocean it would strengthen her legs after the surgery and heal her abscess too. Evelyn could help us. Dr. Krane loves horses. He wouldn't mind at all."

Papa got up and paced the porch once more. "Two surgeries on *a horse,* and now you want to take her to a beach resort."

"I promised Illusion we'd give her a chance to live," Mary pleaded. "What would Mama do?"

He stood gazing out over the porch railing covered with violet flower vines. Flipping his cap at a bee challenging his ownership of the porch, he turned to Mary. "One thing for sure, I'm taking you to Florida to continue your aquatic therapy as soon as I can arrange it."

"We can't go without Illusion." Her eyes pleaded.

Papa appealed to the heavens with one raised arm and a shake of his pointed finger. "Do you see what I have to deal with?"

"Mama would want us to take Illusion."

The curtain fluttered, catching his eye, and a red-eyed, tear-stained Mrs. Tate nodded yes to Papa.

"Guess I'm outmaneuvered and outnumbered." He frowned at his soiled shirt and brushed futilely at the dirt for several long moments. Finally, a soft sigh escaped his lips. "We should make plans to transport Illusion to Florida then."

A cheer erupted from behind the rosebushes.

Papa gasped. "You too, Joe?"

Mary beamed and hugged herself. "She'll need a special horse trailer with a sling to support her after her surgery. I'll ask Laura if we can take Treasure with us to keep Illusion company."

"You know, a little legal issue still needs to be resolved."

"Legal issue?" Mary grimaced in her immediate alarm.

"We don't own her."

Mary's eyes grew huge. "But Laura said..."

"I know. No matter what Laura said, it needs to be finalized. You want her forever, right?"

Mary smiled triumphantly and burst into song. Her arms waved to punctuate her heart's melody. Looking hopefully at Papa, she asked, "Can we go buy her now? We have to tell Illusion and Laura the news."

CHAPTER TWELVE

Six months later, Mary floated in the emerald tidal pool in complete peace and bliss. She opened one eye to peek at Papa. He'd gotten a healthy tan from the last few months near the sea. Papa's new wife, Charlotte, unfolded her fingers to offer him the perfect sand dollar she'd plucked from the white sands as quiet waves lapped the shore.

The surf sparkled in the morning sun. A snort drifted down the beach carried by the ocean breeze. Mary's heart smiled with recognition. Evelyn rode Illusion's best buddy, Treasure, bareback in chest-deep water. Illusion swam along beside him with powerful, steady strokes. Her baby legs stood straight and strong. When Evelyn turned and brought the foal out of the deep water, the little horse squealed and bucked.

"Her happy dance," cried Mary. "Want to see mine?" She squirmed out of the lounge chair in the tidal pool. Scooping arches of emerald water in the air, she celebrated the new strength in her legs.

Papa watched her with a smile in his heart. From a beach bag, he drew out a small wooden bay horse—perfectly restored, just like the precious miracle before him. He extended it to her.

"You had her all along." Mary kissed his cheek. "Thank you." Mary clutched it to her chest. "I love you, Papa." Dancing delicately on the white sands of glory, Mary sang her song—off key, on the top of her lungs.

Dear Reader

The story continues with Mary's granddaughter in
Selah's Sweet Dream.
Please share a review of this book.
Check my website for any ongoing contests or giveaways.
Sign up to be notified of the release of the next horse adventure.
http://www.susancount.com/

E-mail a comment:
susancountauthor@yahoo.com

Follow Susan Count
www.facebook.com/susancount
https://www.pinterest.com/susancount/
https://twitter.com/SusanCount

Award Winning
DREAM HORSE ADVENTURES
Series

MARY'S SONG–BOOK 1

A girl and a foal share one thing. They are both lame. One cannot survive without the other.

SELAH'S SWEET DREAM–BOOK 2

A girl with a dream to be an equestrian superstar. A horse with ATTITUDE.

SELAH'S PAINTED DREAM–BOOK 3

One word can ruin a perfect life—moving.

SELAH'S STOLEN DREAM–BOOK 4

One girl's victory is the other's tragic defeat.

READER REVIEWS:

Best horse books ever. Charming. Action packed. Heart-warming. Page turner. I'm utterly smitten. Stole my heart. Good for the soul.

ABOUT WRITING...

One day...I began to write with no preconceived ideas about anything. I'd read what I had written the day before and add another scene to the adventure. No one could have been more astounded than I was when it turned into a book, then two books. The whole process gave me great joy and restored my spirit after a season of loss. My motivation was my desire  to bless one particular young lady with a story to show her a love relationship in a family, with the Lord and with a horse. I truly thought the story would remain in a drawer until she was old enough to read it. Surprise!

I write at an antique secretary desk, which belonged to the same grandmother who introduced me to horse books. The desk has secret compartments and occupies a glass room with a forest view. Bunnies and cardinals regularly interrupt my muse, as do my horses grazing in a clearing.

Though I am a rider and lover of horses, I make no claims of expertise in any riding discipline. I hope my research keeps me from annoying those who would know.

The only thing more fun than riding might be writing horse adventure stories.

Saddle up and ride along!

Made in the USA
Middletown, DE
10 April 2020

88896777R00068